Girls on Film

A-List novels by Zoey Dean

THE A-LIST
GIRLS ON FILM
BLONDE AMBITION
TALL COOL ONE
BACK IN BLACK
SOME LIKE IT HOT
AMERICAN BEAUTY
HEART OF GLASS
BEAUTIFUL STRANGER

If you like THE A-LIST, you may also enjoy:

Bass Ackwards and Belly Up by Elizabeth Craft and Sarah Fain
Secrets of My Hollywood Life by Jen Calonita
Haters by Alisa Valdes-Rodriguez
Betwixt by Tara Bray Smith
Poseur by Rachel Maude

Girls on Film

An A-List Novel

by
Zoey Dean

poppy

LITTLE, BROWN AND COMPANY
New York   Boston

Poppy

Little, Brown and Company
Hachette Book Group USA
237 Park Avenue, New York, NY 10017
For more of your favorite series, go to www.pickapoppy.com

First Edition: April 2004

The Poppy name and logo are trademarks of Hachette Book Group USA.

alloyentertainment

Produced by Alloy Entertainment
151 West 26th Street, New York, NY 10001

Cover design by Marci Senders
Cover photography (foreground image) copyright Pure/Nonstock
Cover photography (background image) copyright Ken Biggs/Stone

ISBN 978-0-316-73475-2

10 9 8 7 6

CWO

Printed in the United States of America

Love is a fire. But whether it is going to warm your hearth or burn down your house, you can never tell.

—Joan Crawford

Prologue

Susan Cabot Percy was reasonably sure there was a time when she'd been as innocent and virginal as her younger sister, Anna. But that time seemed long ago and far away. So long ago that it felt like a life that belonged to someone else.

"Whoa! Awesome!"

This from the male body next to her.

Susan tried to recall his name. Blue? Red? It was a color, that much she remembered. And the name was also associated with some old folk-rock musician, because when he'd checked in that morning and introduced himself, he'd made a lame joke to her about it.

Brown. Like the color. That was it. His name was Brown. Neither his hair, eyes, nor skin was remotely close to the color he was named after, so his parents couldn't have chosen it based on looks. Not that she cared why Brown was called Brown. Susan didn't really know him, didn't want to know him, and planned never to know him, except in the biblical sense. Granted, sex with strangers was risky (even with the proper precautions), but a girl had to do something with her free time.

Copious free time, actually. Because Susan was finding alcohol and drug rehabilitation at Minneapolis's famous Hazelden clinic to be excruciatingly boring. She always skipped group therapy because she had zero desire to share her personal life with the flotsam and jetsam who happened to be at the facility with her. And supervised outings weren't exactly her idea of fun. They reminded her of her preschool days at the 92nd Street Y in New York City (a place impossible to get into unless your last name was Vanderbilt or Lodge. Or Percy).

"Damn, I got a mean-ass crick in my neck," Brown complained, rubbing a spot just above his collarbone. He rolled over onto a stack of towels that had fallen during their tryst.

Susan knew that the linen closet wasn't exactly conducive to a relaxing encounter. But she'd picked it for privacy, not comfort. It was after midnight. The housekeepers were all gone for the day. Towels and sheets for residents had long been distributed and counted, so no one was going to come looking for extras. And the linen closet was more comfortable than the basement bathroom, which had been her other option for this rendezvous.

"You want a hit?" Brown asked. His eyes were such a vibrant shade of green, the color was even discernable in the dim light of the closet.

"Hit" could refer to either the hash-filled bong by his side or the half-pint of Jose Cuervo that he was nursing. How he'd managed to sneak in the contraband was another thing Susan didn't care about.

"No thanks." Something about Hazelden must be

working because Susan had been clean and sober since her arrival. There was no reason to ruin her record for Brown. Candy and cigarettes, however, only filled so much of the void left by the alcohol and pills she'd banished from her life. And while it was prohibited, at least sex didn't make you fat or give you cancer.

Susan rolled over and regarded Brown as he torched the bong and launched into some navel-gazing story about how his overbearing parents had forced him into rehab. He was a few years younger than her—maybe even still in high school—and very cute, in a blond, surfer dude sort of way. But they were strangers in the night and she planned to keep it that way. She could have launched into her own tale of woe, of course. Poor little rich girl and the uptight, Social Register parents who had done her wrong. Been there, whined that.

Susan checked her watch and realized it was only around 10:30 P.M. in Beverly Hills, California, where her sister, Anna, was now living. Anna was the only person she felt like talking to. Anna was the only person she *could* talk to, about anything remotely important. But all day long she'd left endless messages on her sister's cell. Anna hadn't called her back. Susan didn't want to admit how much that hurt.

". . . So I decided to head to Maui with my buddy, and I go to take some cash out of my account, and check this out: My parents had the account frozen, if you can believe that shit," Brown droned.

God, he was excruciating. Either she had to shut him

up or go back to her room. But her middle-aged room-mate, Vanessa, had insomnia and stayed up all night obsessing over her stock portfolio, eschewing both laptop and PalmPilot to do complex calculations by hand in a ledger book with a fountain pen. If that wasn't freaky enough, Vanessa was one of those born-again rehabbers who felt it was her personal mission to report any infraction of the rules. The day that Susan had been assigned to clean their bathroom after Vanessa's ablutions, Vanessa had evaluated her work with a ten-point checklist. Susan had told Vanessa where she could stuff her ledgers. They weren't exactly bestest friends.

She could have another go at Brown Boy, she supposed. Or watch a DVD. Or try to figure out how a girl as smart and cute and rich as she knew herself to be had, at the ripe old age of twenty, gone utterly wrong. Or—

The door swung open. There stood Vanessa, blue-tinged sheets in hand, one arm covered in blue ink. She took in the sight of Brown and Susan in what was an extremely compromising position.

"I spilled ink," she said by way of explanation.

"Yeah, fine, we're cool, right?" Brown asked, trying for a casual cover-up of the tequila bottle, the bong, and himself with a stray pillowcase. It failed miserably.

Vanessa might be a lot of things—some of which required antipsychotic medication—but cool was not one of them. She had never been cool, and she never would be cool. She had pimples on her back and bad hair and breasts the size of raisins and a midlevel management job at a Fortune 500 company. Susan, on the other hand, was blond, curvaceous, and wealthy enough never to work unless she wanted to.

In other words, she was everything that Vanessa was not. In other words, defender-of-the-Hazelden-flame Vanessa was sure to blow the whistle; the Hazelden administration would know about Susan's transgressions before sunrise. That she had not indulged in the contraband would be no defense. Susan knew the rules. She was there. The drugs and alcohol were there, too. Which meant, Susan knew only too well, she'd soon be outta there on her ass.

And to make matters worse, Brown Boy was *so* not worth it.

Daisy Buchanan Meets Daisy Duke

Ben *who?*
  This was Anna Percy's mantra to get her through her first day at Beverly Hills High School. Just seventy-two hours earlier—New Year's Eve, in fact—she'd met Ben Birnbaum on a flight from New York to Los Angeles. She'd been on her way west to live with her father for the last semester of her senior year of high school. Ben was a freshman at Princeton coming home for a wedding. Also, he was hot, funny, and smart. The kind of guy you dream exists, if you're a dreamy sort of girl.

Anna was many things: tall, blond, well educated, and very wealthy, with a passion for literature and the poems of Emily Dickinson. What she was not, by anyone's standards (least of all her own), was dreamy. Or impetuous. That was why it had felt like an out-of-body experience when, merely an hour after encountering Ben in the first-class cabin of their transcontinental flight, she'd found herself making out with him in the lavatory, dangerously close to flying United.

Anna had come to Los Angeles in the hopes of

reinventing herself, and Ben had seemed the perfect boy with whom to debut the new and daring her. But now, when she considered everything that had happened with Ben between the heavenly plane flight and the hellish conclusion, Anna was convinced, more than ever, that her usually impeccable taste did not extend to guys.

There was no pretty way to put it: Ben had dumped her at 3:00 A.M. on New Year's Day. Disappeared without a trace, only to show up two days later begging for forgiveness. He'd had to go rescue some mystery celebrity friend. Female, of course. He wouldn't share her name.

That was his excuse. The more Anna thought about it, the more pissed off she got. It was true that Ben knew a lot of celebrities—she'd seen dozens of them at the wedding they'd attended together. But still. It was all just so ridiculous, such an insult to her intelligence. She'd been a fool for Ben. And Anna Percy was nobody's fool.

"Anna! Cool! I was hoping we'd have at least one class together."

Samantha Sharpe smiled broadly at Anna from the next row of seats, showing off ten thousand dollars' worth of pearly crowned perfection. Her brown hair glistened in a way that's only possible with a professional blowout.

"Sam. Hi." Anna had been raised well by her patrician mother back in New York City—she was an expert at looking pleased while her insides were registering anything but pleasure. So she returned Sam's smile. They'd met at the New Year's Eve wedding—Sam's father, Jackson Sharpe, America's best-loved movie star, had been the groom. That night she'd also met Sam's two best friends, Dee Young, the daughter of a big-time record exec, and Cammie Sheppard, the daughter of a feared and revered Hollywood *über*-agent. They were oh-so-friendly at first. But it hadn't taken long for them to show their true colors.

Well, Anna thought, *if I have to be in a class with one of them, Sam is certainly the least offensive—*

At that moment Dee and Cammie sashayed through the door of Anna's last class of the day, English. All three snouts of Cerebus present and accounted for. Damn.

"Hi, Anna. How was day one?" diminutive Dee chirped as she took a seat directly behind Sam's.

"Fine."

"You know, I looked for you at lunch," Sam told Anna. "We went to Westside Pavilion for sushi and I wanted to invite you." Evidently the girls were in friendly mode.

"I went for a walk," Anna explained.

Cammie took a seat in front of Sam, swept her strawberry blond curls over her shoulder, and eyed Anna coolly. "Just out of idle curiosity, why are you dressed like that?"

Anna felt the prickly heat of a blush on the back of her neck. Back in Manhattan, torn and decrepit were considered hip. For her first day at Beverly Hills High

School she'd put on a "normal" school outfit: a white T-shirt, a camel cashmere cardigan with a moth hole on the sleeve, and battered jeans. She'd pulled her long, silky blond hair into a simple ponytail and dabbed on a little Burt's Bees cherry-flavored lip balm. That Anna could make this look terrific had everything to do with genetics and upbringing.

The three girls, though, were walking examples of Anna's observation that in Beverly Hills, when it came to cosmetics, more was more, and when it came to square inches of flesh covered by designer fabric, more was less. Each of them sported so much lip gloss it looked as if one could skate across their lips. They each wore very small, very expensive sweaters with their extremely low slung pants and stiletto-heeled boots.

Of the three, pear-shaped Sam tried the hardest but had the least to work with. Dee got by on her big-eyed, shaggy blond, tiny preciousness. And Cammie . . . well, Cammie looked like the kind of girl who'd be featured in a men's magazine with a staple in her navel. Her white sweater stopped more than four inches short of her cargo pants. Somehow she'd acquired a tan since Anna had first met her, which set off her lush I-just-had-insane-sex curls to perfection. Anna had learned on New Year's Eve that Ben Birnbaum and Cammie had been a couple last year; Cammie had made it more than clear that she wanted Ben back.

Anna willed away her blush. "I wasn't aware that I had to run my clothes by you for approval."

"Just a tidbit of advice," Cammie said, unfazed. "Don't drink coffee from a paper cup. Someone might drop a quarter into it."

"Give it a rest, Cammie," Sam suggested.

Anna was surprised. Sam hadn't struck her as secure enough to stand up to Cammie. But then, being the famous Jackson Sharpe's daughter had to count for something. There were times when Anna had thought maybe Sam could be a friend. But since Anna could never be sure if Sam was moving in for a hug or a mugging, it made friendship a bit dicey.

Sam turned back to Anna. "We really do have to go shopping. We can hit the boutiques on Rodeo, but it has to be sometime when the tourists aren't out. I so cannot deal with the primates at fashion feeding time."

"I don't need clothes, Sam," Anna said. "Thanks anyway."

The bell rang. Their English teacher, Mrs. Breckner, a middle-aged woman in an unfortunate floral pants ensemble, closed the door. "I'm sure you all read *The Great Gatsby* over winter break," she began, "between gin-and-tonics in Aruba and powder runs at Mammoth."

A few kids chuckled at the teacher's dry wit. Others rolled their eyes or just looked bored. Mrs. Breckner launched into a lecture on the major themes in *Gatsby*, stopping every so often to pose a question. Anna didn't volunteer any answers, though she certainly knew them all—she'd first read the Fitzgerald classic when she was thirteen.

"Rather than having you write the usual papers," Mrs. Breckner went on, "let's try something new and different. I'm going to have you pair up and create a presentation project on the book. Write a short play, make a sculpture, do a performance piece, whatever speaks to you.

"Don't take the text literally, people," she added. "We're dealing with broad themes there—old wealth versus new wealth, individualism and self-discovery versus easy money and group-think. Okay, everyone in row one choose someone from row two; same thing for rows three and four."

"How about it, Anna?" Sam asked. "Partners?"

Anna was too polite to say no. Besides, Sam seemed like a better option than a completely unknown quantity. "Sure," she said. "That would be great."

"Any brilliant ideas?"

"Not immediately."

"How about a short film?" Sam suggested. "I'm thinking a clash-of-the-classes kinda thing. Daisy Buchanan meets Daisy Duke. At a party."

"That sounds promising," Anna said. "Maybe we could we give this party? Mix actors and real people? And film it?"

Sam tapped a finger on her lips thoughtfully. "Dunno. Haven't thought it through. We should talk later, okay? I'll call you."

"Fine."

Then Anna remembered that she'd chucked her cell

phone that morning because Ben wouldn't stop calling her.

No. She was not, not, not going to think about Ben. Or rather, *Ben who?*

"Don't use my cell," Anna added. "I'm . . . changing numbers." She quickly scribbled her father's home number on a piece of paper.

Sam slipped the paper into her Chanel purse, then fiddled with the top button of her paisley Stella McCartney sweater. "You know, I've been meaning to ask you: Didn't I see Ben Birnbaum here this morning, talking to you?"

Anna shrugged. She did *not* want to get into this with Sam.

"He looked awful," Sam went on, undeterred. "Like he'd been up all night partying or something. What's up with that? I'm only asking you because I'm concerned."

"I have no idea," Anna replied, hoping the frost in her voice would dissuade Sam. It didn't.

"Did he tell you why he hasn't gone back to Princeton yet? I know classes started."

"I really don't want to talk about Ben."

"Please," Sam scoffed. "You've known him, what, three days? I've known him my whole life. So you might as well tell me, because I'm going to find out anyway."

"If you and Ben are such good friends, Sam, ask him yourself."

Sam raised her perfectly-shaped-by-Valerie eyebrows. "Touchy, touchy."

What the hell, Anna thought. "Look, Sam, if you're asking me whether Ben and I are seeing each other, the answer is no."

A joy that Anna could not understand suffused Sam's face. "Are you saying that you *broke up* with Ben Birnbaum?" Sam asked, grabbing Anna's arm.

Anna shrugged off Sam's hand. "We had one date. There wasn't anything to break up."

The bell rang to end the school day; Anna retrieved her books and her purse. As she departed, she saw Sam huddle with Cammie and Dee. Anna refused to care. If they want to obsess over Ben, that was their business. She was over him.

But . . .

As Anna dodged bodies on her way out of the classroom, a little voice in the back of her brain kept asking the niggling question, If she was so over him, why the hell did she need to keep thinking about how much she was over him?

High School for the Highly Overprivileged

"Whoa, careful! Planet hopping?"

As Anna stepped into the crowded hallway, she nearly collided with Adam Flood, another person she'd met at the Jackson Sharpe nuptials. Anna liked him more than anyone else she'd met so far in Beverly Hills. Maybe it was because, like Anna, he was a transplant, having come to California two years earlier from Michigan. Fortunately, his seven-hundred-odd days of exposure to the rarefied air of Beverly Hills hadn't seemed to affect his refreshing midwestern lack of artifice. He was also tall and lanky, sweet and smart, and allegedly an ace basketball player.

"Sorry, I was thinking," Anna said as Adam fell in beside her. They headed for the door closest to the student parking lot.

"Good thinking, bad thinking, none-of-the-above thinking?"

She smiled up at him. He had a small blue star tattoo behind his left ear that was very cute. "I was thinking about how nice it is to see you, actually."

"*Definitely* good thinking," Adam said. "So how was your first day at Beverly Hills High School for the Highly Overprivileged?"

"Mixed reviews. American lit was okay. Chem was good, until my lab mate gave me a blow-by-blow of her seduction of a sitcom star. And I mean that literally."

"Don't tell me. Shakti Carter." Adam held the door open for her and they stepped into the afternoon sun.

She laughed. "How did you know?"

"She's famous for 'oversharing,' if you know what I mean. What do you think of Breckner?"

Anna shrugged. "I like her. I'm working on a *Gatsby* project with Sam."

They strolled across the parking lot, where everyone seemed to be getting into their Porsches or BMWs. "Sam's smart," Adam said.

"Yeah, I got that. I almost feel like we could be friends, but . . ."

"Ah, the infamous *but*," Adam joked.

"There are her two appendages to consider."

"Dee and Cammie," Adam filled in. "Little Girl Lost and Not So Little Girl Even More Lost."

"This is me," Anna said when they reached the pearl-gray Lexus that Anna's father had leased for her. She shielded her eyes from the sun with her right hand. "Dee, maybe. But Cammie Sheppard? She strikes me as something of a barracuda."

Adam scratched his tattoo. "Yeah, she puts up a good front, I admit. But she hasn't had an easy go of it.

Did you know her mom died in a freak accident? Her stepmother hates her, and her father's nuts. I think she's worse off than Dee."

"Don't you ever say anything mean to anyone?"

"Oh, yeah," Adam replied, eyeing Anna's car. "How about, 'Damn girl, you've got one fine-ass ride and you're the only one in it. Didn't you ever hear about conserving energy?'"

Anna smiled. "Is that a hint you'd like a ride home?"

Adam plunged an invisible dagger into his heart. "Painful as it is to admit, I'm pretty sure I'm the only senior with a *b* word. As in bicycle. Don't let it get around."

Annie held up her palm. "Promise."

"I usually scrounge a ride with someone," Adam added.

"Just call me someone," Anna quipped. "Hop in."

Adam opened the door for her, then went around to his side and got into the car. Between the balmy afternoon and Adam sitting next to her, Anna started to feel better about life as she pulled onto Sunset Boulevard. Happy, even.

A car horn beeped. Anna turned to see a classic cherry-red Jensen Interceptor, top down, in the lane to her right. Sam was behind the wheel, Cammie in the passenger seat, and Dee in the back. "You two look really cute together!" Sam shouted mockingly. Cammie gave them a laconic wave. "Talk to you later!"

"Well, it's better than the finger," Adam remarked,

taking in Cammie's salute. "I think she's jealous that you got Ben. They used to be a couple."

"So I've been told. But to clarify things, I don't in any way, shape, or form 'have Ben.' Nor has Ben *had* me." Her eyes flicked to Adam, then back to the road.

"Turn right on Rexford and go toward Coldwater. So . . . you're not madly, passionately in love with Ben Birnbaum?"

"I don't even like him, Adam."

"Really?" Adam's eyes lit up.

"Really. Why is that such a surprise?"

"Know how there's one guy at every school every girl seems to want? I think God doles 'em out. Ben was that guy last year. And the year before that."

"Well, then, I guess I'm not every girl."

"Good to know. Slow down. My house is on the right, with the hoop in the driveway." Anna pulled in and stopped. Adam swiveled to her. "So. Thanks for the ride."

"You're welcome."

Adam drummed his long, narrow fingers on the dashboard. "So . . ."

It appeared to Anna that Adam wanted to say something, but she couldn't quite figure out what it was. She waited patiently. It was the well-bred thing to do.

"Do you like dogs?" Adam blurted.

That's what he wanted to say? "Sure."

He nodded. "I've got one."

"What kind?"

"Serious Heinz. You know. Fifty-seven varieties of

mutt. Name's Bowser. I adopted him right after we moved here."

That was a nice thing to do, Anna thought. More waiting and more finger drumming. "So . . . ," Adam finally said. "I'm taking him for a run later. Out by Gladstone's. You know it?"

Anna shook her head. "What's Gladstone's?"

"Seafood restaurant between Santa Monica and Pacific Palisades. A ton of tourists, but the beach is lit. I thought if you weren't doing anything, maybe you'd like to come along. Just to hang out."

Was Adam asking her out? As in a date? Or did he mean "hang out" in the just-friends sense? Huh. She hadn't given him a moment's thought as a possible romance because her head had been too full of—

Shut up, head, she scolded herself. "Sounds like fun," she agreed.

"Yeah? Wow. Cool. Oh, dress warm. It gets chilly out there after dark. I'll pick you up at . . . six, okay?"

"With what?" Anna asked. "I thought you didn't have a car."

"If I call my mom at her office and grovel, she might let me borrow hers. She and my dad commute to work together—they have for years. It's almost too sweet to witness." He got out and waved as Anna pulled out of his driveway.

During the five minutes it took Anna to drive to her dad's house, she thought about what a truly nice guy Adam was. The kind of guy she *should* be dating.

Should.

But Anna hadn't moved three thousand miles for "should."

Anna saw them the moment she pulled into the circular drive of her father's house. The elegant house, built by Anna's grandparents in the 1950s, was massive. White stucco with red shutters, shaded by giant palm and eucalyptus trees. Crimson, pink, purple, and lavender flowers flanked the path to the front door. And today, for extra-added fun, the redbrick front walkway just happened to be lined with hundreds of red and white helium balloons, strings anchored by beanbags on the ground.

She stopped the car, got out, and followed the balloon-lined walkway to the front door. Three more balloons were tied to the handle, and taped to the biggest balloon was an envelope. Anna removed the envelope; in the process the three balloons floated off. She watched them bob into the sky, remembering the last time she'd let helium balloons go free. She'd been six, walking with her parents in New York's Central Park on a hot summer afternoon. She, her mom, and her dad had all written self-addressed postcards and taped them to balloons, asking the finder to please write on the card where the balloon had landed and drop the card in a mailbox.

There'd been an odd east wind that July day, and the balloons had flown west toward the Hudson River. Two days later they'd gotten a postcard back from an old man in Passaic, New Jersey, who'd found one of the balloons dangling from a maple tree in his backyard. It was one of the more vivid memories Anna had of her family when it had seemed happy and whole.

When the balloons were pinpricks against the California blue, Anna opened the envelope.

> *ANNA—*
>   *I SCREWED UP. PLEASE FORGIVE ME.*
> *I NEED TO SEE YOU.*
>   *—BEN*

Damn him.

Damn him to hell. Why was he doing something sweet and wonderful? And why was she falling for it?

"If I can stop one heart from breaking, I shall not live in vain. . . ."

The line from an Emily Dickinson poem came to mind as she commanded herself to harden her heart. If Ben Birnbaum thought she could be seduced by a bunch of balloons and a pleading note, he was sorely mistaken. No matter what Anna felt for him, no matter how drawn she was to him, no matter how good he could make her feel, she knew he was bad for her. His gesture was sweet on the outside. But there was no telling what was driving him on the inside.

Anna spotted some pruning shears outside the garage door and used them to release each of Ben's balloons to the heavens—a place Anna was sure that Ben would never be admitted.

I Wanna Be Sedated

Samantha Sharpe was drinking tea. And Samantha Sharpe was not happy.

Her movie-star father and his pregnant new wife, Poppy Sharpe (the former Poppy Sinclair, who was now emphatically using her new husband's surname), were having afternoon tea in the five-hundred-square-foot formal dining room of the Sharpe family twelve-thousand-square-foot Bel Air mansion. Thanks to the New Year's Eve nuptials, Poppy was now Sam's stepmother, and the trio were calling said mansion home sweet home.

Logically, Jackson Sharpe and his new bride should still have been on their honeymoon to Sandy Lane in Barbados. But they hadn't been on the Caribbean island for more than one night when Poppy had awakened in hysterics; she was feeling insecure so far away from Beverly Hills and her obstetrician. Jackson had tried to reason with her; the baby wasn't due for another eight weeks. But Poppy wasn't buying what Jackson was selling. What if something in the exotic diet triggered early labor? What if they didn't have the really good drugs that she absolutely had to have when she went into labor?

So they'd chartered a jet and come back to Los Angeles, which was why Sam was currently bonding with the newest member of her family over cranberry and orange muffins, raspberry scones with clotted cream, and fresh papaya.

Poppy loved afternoon tea. She'd read that afternoon tea was served at Buckingham Palace. Poppy's grandmother had been British. For Poppy, that was connection enough to the royals—she ordered that afternoon tea become a Sharpe household institution. Sam had experienced a moment of intestinal distress when she'd come home from school to find that her father and Poppy had ditched their honeymoon. But what could she do? Her father beckoned her to join them over the tissue-paper-thin teacups, so she did. The sight of Poppy sitting there with that humungous Harry Winston diamond on the ring finger of her left hand, which was resting on her humungously pregnant belly, was enough to make Sam shovel down the scones. (It turned out that she was the only one who consumed them. At the last moment Poppy decided that they were too rich and stuck to tea and dry sprouted-wheat bread. As for Jackson Sharpe, he was starting a new movie at the end of the month called *Glamour Boys*, about the party scene in the eighties. He was to play an AIDS patient and had to lose fifteen pounds before the start of principal photography. All he had for afernoon tea was tea.)

"The whole family! This is so nice," Poppy cooed, and blew a kiss across the table to her groom. He blew one back.

Sam swallowed the last of her third scone, beyond appalled. Her stepmother—minus the belly bump— looked like a Laker Girl. Permatan, legs that never ended, bleached blond hair, and boob-o-licious. Plus she was only four years older than Sam. Talk about your horrific Hollywood clichés.

Sam, a budding film director, often thought of her life as a movie, complete with music score. Her plan was to do for this decade what Scorcese had done for the seventies. What would work now? Maybe something old and punk? "I Wanna Be Sedated"? No. *No* Ramones. They were using their music in AT&T commercials now. Dead Kennedys, maybe. "Too Drunk to . . ." If only her father had taken that song literally. Then Sam wouldn't be looking at acquiring a half-sister or half-brother in a couple of months.

As Sam chewed, Poppy frowned. "I hope you're not binging and purging, Sam. Because I had a friend who ruptured something and nearly died from that."

About fifteen different responses ran through Sam's mind, but she choked them all down in favor of the neutral. "Thanks for sharing."

"Sam . . . watch the tone," her father said in between sips of tea.

Apparently not neutral enough.

Poppy looked self-righteous, and Sam gave her a

withering look, thinking again how this marriage made no sense. As America's most popular movie star, Jackson Sharpe could have his pick of women. He almost always ended up in a fling with whatever barely-old-enough-to-vote ingénue was in his latest film. When the movie ended, so did the romance. Sam figured her father must be very careful about birth control because if he wasn't—at the rate he changed girlfriends—he'd have enough off-spring by now to form his own Little League team.

So what had happened with this girl? How had Poppy managed to get pregnant and get Jackson to marry her?

Then Sam had a cheery thought: What if Poppy's bun in the oven belonged to someone else? Maybe she could figure out a way to get the baby's DNA tested. If the baby *wasn't* her father's, maybe Jackson would dump Poppy's ass, and she wouldn't have to lose what little attention her father gave her to some drooling, burping poop machine with Poppy's perfect jawline.

"So, Sam, how's everything going?" her father asked.

Well, at least it was an attempt at showing interest.

"Okay."

"Great, kitten." He slapped his flat abdomen. "I'm in for a killer workout. Billy Blanks is coming over to whip me into shape." He checked his Cellini Quartz Rolex and backed away from the table. She tried to think of something that would keep him at the table a little longer.

"I'm making a short film, Dad. For a school assignment."

"That's great, babe."

He already sounded distracted. Not good. "With my friend Anna, from New York. She's really nice—I want you to meet her."

"Uh-huh." He patted the crown of his head to make sure his hair covered the spot that was starting to go bald.

"A sort of Gatsby meets Fellini meets the Beverly Hillbillies thing," Sam rushed on. "So I'll need to give a party, probably Saturday night. And film it."

"Saturday?" Poppy echoed.

"Yes, Poppy," Sam said slowly. "You know, the day after Friday."

"I *meant* that our renovations are beginning this weekend. So a party would be out of the question."

Sam turned to her father. "Renovations?"

"I told Poppy she could do whatever she wants to with the place," her father said pleasantly. "She doesn't feel at home here yet, and she wants to outfit one of the upstairs rooms for the baby. The one next to yours, in fact."

Sam could practically hear the incessant wail of a colicky baby at three o'clock in the morning. "I think we're fine. I don't want the house redecorated. Well, maybe a little soundproofing."

"Hey, sugarbun, you're off to college next year. You won't even be living here. But for us, it's forever." Her father went around the table and kissed his new wife.

"Sam's sorry, Poppy. We all need a little time to adjust to our new family. So what about you today?"

"I'm meeting with my life coach to work on names for the baby. I'm thinking Chrysalis if it's a girl. Isn't that pretty?"

Yeah, Sam thought. *Except you wouldn't be able to spell it.*

"Then I'm having lunch with Lateesha Allison," Poppy went on. "We might do a CD together."

"Great, sweetheart," Jackson said distractedly as he checked his hair in the mirror over the buffet table.

"Poppy, Lateesha Allison had a number-one single last year," Sam pointed out. "Why would she do a duet with you?"

"Your father set it up. I happen to have a trained voice, Sam."

That was it.

There was only so long that she could sit there and listen to this airhead pretend she had anything going for her *other* than her marriage to an Oscar winner. Sam stood up, said she had homework to do, and headed for the stairs.

She'd just have to pin all her hopes on the DNA test.

Existential Funk

"Hi, Anna."

Anna's father, Jonathan Percy, stood in the doorway leading to the palatial living room. Tall and rangy, wearing battered jeans and an ancient blue T-shirt, he easily looked ten years younger than he was. It was strange, because Anna had always known her dad to be a Savile Row suit kind of guy, consumed by his work as one of the country's leading investment analysts—a guy who worked on Christmas because they didn't celebrate in the Asian markets. But in the three days since she'd come to California, he'd mostly been scruffing around in jeans and tees, smelling more than faintly of marijuana.

"Dad. I didn't expect you to be home." Anna swung her leather backpack off her shoulder and set it on the antique rustic French side table. A different Ming vase had already replaced the one she'd accidentally shattered on New Year's Eve. She'd run into it in the pitch-black foyer and sent it crashing to the marble-tiled floor.

"I worked from home today," he explained. "How was school?"

Anna shrugged. "Honestly? A waste of time. We got assigned *Gatsby* in lit class. I read it when I was in eighth grade."

Jonathan nodded. "They're probably teaching to some standardized test. Look, I know the internship I lined up for you at Randall Prescott's agency fell through, but I've got something else cooking."

She sighed, not feeling hopeful. "Thanks. I made a bunch of calls yesterday and faxed my resume everywhere. Maybe I'll hear something, too. I guess I'll go upstairs and do my homework. I'm going out later."

"Can you come into the kitchen? I want to talk to you about something."

Her first instinct was to make some excuse as to why this wasn't a good time for a heart-to-heart. Avoiding confrontation was a knee-jerk reaction instilled by Anna's mother, who referred to any encounter with an emotional component as "making a scene." But part of Anna's motivation for coming to Los Angeles had been to take the opportunity to get to know the father who'd left Anna's life when she was only seven. The split had been so hostile, he'd been forced to leave his wife with not only the Manhattan duplex but full custody of the children *and* the entire East Coast.

So she followed her dad into the spotless, ultramodern kitchen. There was a stainless-steel center island for cooking, a restaurant-quality double oven against one wall, and a red Swedish table and matching chairs that could have easily fit in the design wing of the Museum of Modern

Art. For once, none of the household staff was lurking.

Her father peered inside the refrigerator. "Sparkling water? Soy milk? Juice?"

Anna was surprised. The cook seemed to purchase what she needed on a daily basis, which left the refrigerator empty. "Since when do we have cold beverages?"

"Since I had Gelson's deliver groceries. What can I get you?"

"Juice is fine. Any kind." Anna took a seat as her dad poured pear juice into two Baccarat crystal goblets and handed one to Anna

"So, how's your mom?"

She was what he wanted to talk about?

"Still in Italy," Anna said, keeping her voice neutral. "I haven't spoken to her since the last time you asked me. Yesterday."

"I thought the two of you kept in really good touch." He stood near the cooking console, as if reluctant to sit.

Anna shrugged. "I have her phone number. If you're so interested in how she's doing, call her."

"Somehow I doubt that's a call she'd welcome." He gulped down the last of his juice.

"Well, from what I've heard, you didn't show much interest in her when the two of you were married, so it might be odd to start after you've been divorced for ten years." Anna knew that sounded harsher than she'd intended. But her father had intimated that he wanted to talk about her. Instead, this was all about him.

"I was a jerk back then." Finally he took a seat

kitty-corner from Anna and stretched his long legs out under the table. "People change, though."

"Good to know."

Her father wagged a finger at her but grinned gamely. "I know that tone. That's the patented Jane Percy frost-on-the-voice."

"The apple doesn't fall far from the tree, I guess."

He nodded, turning the goblet between his fingers. "Anna, I really am working on lining up another internship for you. I want you to know that."

"Thanks. That's nice of you."

"But you sound like you're talking to a stranger."

"Well, we kind of are strangers," Anna pointed out.

Her dad scratched his chin. "Touché. So I should know tomorrow if it's happening. It might be an after-school internship, though. You'll still have to go to classes. Sorry about that."

"Can I ask where?"

"Margaret is leaving her agency to help start up a new one. I think they're going to call it Apex. They'll have some actors, but the main focus is going to be setting up novels and plays for the movies. Their long-term goal is to open a New York office and do books, too."

Margaret was Anna's dad's girlfriend. It was no surprise to Anna that her dad was romantically involved with someone. What was surprising was that she wasn't a Hollywood starlet wannabe, but a woman in her forties who was a dead ringer for Anna's mom.

Anna grimaced. "I appreciate the effort, Dad. But I

really don't want to intern with your . . . relationship."

"If you'd take the time to get to know Margaret, you'd like her. She's like your mom in a lot of ways, but nicer."

"Ouch."

Jonathan smiled. "I do value your loyalty. Anyway, you won't be working with her, specifically. If it works out, it'll be with all three partners. I'll let you know as soon as I hear something."

"I appreciate that, I really do. So, how are you feeling these days?"

Jonathan looked puzzled. "Oh! You mean the headaches I've been having. Not so bad." He frowned. "Except for a killer one yesterday."

"You're still . . . self-medicating?" Anna asked, referring to the lingering odor of pot that even now trailed her dad.

"Only until my doctor gets back from Hawaii," Jonathan told her, noticing his daughter's concerned face. "Don't worry, that's next week. I don't let anyone else touch me." His voice dropped confidentially. "He's the one who suggested my 'medication.'"

"Don't miss your appointment," Anna counseled. "I know how busy you get."

"I've got two secretaries and an assistant to remind me—"

He was cut off by the ringing of his cell phone. "Jonathan Percy," he answered, and listened for a moment. "Hey! Great to hear from you!" He smiled and mouthed to Anna, "It's your sister!"

Anna's sister, Susan, was currently three weeks into her latest rehab stint. Alcohol was her poison of choice, though other illegal substances had been known to find their way down her throat, up her nose, or into her veins. When Susan stayed sober, she and Anna had a great relationship. The problem was—for the last few years, at least—Susan never stayed sober for very long.

Her father was frowning now. He pushed the phone at Anna. "She wants to speak to you," he said coldly.

Anna took the phone, wondering what her sister had just said that had so angered their dad. "Sooz?"

"Hey, I've been calling your cell all day. Don't you check your voice mail?"

"Oh, sorry, I . . . lost my phone," Anna said, since it was too complicated to explain.

"God, I'm reduced to calling our so-called father." Susan shuddered. "How can you stand living with him?"

Anna flicked her eyes at her father, who was watching her with great intensity. She couldn't understand why Susan was suddenly so furious with him. Yes, he'd neglected them. But his had been sins of omission, not commission. Plus it seemed like change was possible. On New Year's Day, Jonathan had called Susan in rehab and told her how much he wanted to repair their relationship.

"Everything's fine," Anna said.

"Bull," Susan spat.

"Is this what you called to tell me?"

Now her sister laughed. "No, you brat. I just wanted to say that Hazelden gave me back my phone privileges, and you're the first person I'm calling."

Anna grinned. Aside from her animosity toward their

dad—which was an ongoing thing—Susan sounded good. Maybe this was the time that rehab would actually work for more than a few months. "So how's it going there, Sooz?"

"Fine."

"No, really," Anna insisted. "Tell me."

"I'm *fine*, big sis," Susan teased.

Anna laughed. Even though Susan was two years older than her, Susan often joked that Anna acted like the older sister. "You sound better than you did the last time we spoke."

"I was in an existential funk, questioning the meaning of life, all that. Plus I was coming down from a sugar high. Four Snickers bars with a root beer chaser."

"Lovely."

"Well, at least I've started working out again. That feels good. So listen, get a new cell so I can call you, okay? You have my number."

"Okay, tomorrow," Anna promised. "You really do sound a lot better, Sooz."

"Hey, I'm the never-say-die girl. So, how long are you hanging at Dad's?"

"I don't know. Awhile. I'm going to Beverly Hills High."

"Well, doesn't that suck."

"Yes, actually," Anna agreed.

"So you're not, like, leaving anytime soon?" Susan asked.

What was this about? "No. Why?"

"So I know where to *reach* you, Anna."

"Here."

"There. Right. Got it. Okay. Love you, little sis. Talk to you soon."

Anna handed the phone back to her father. "Did you have a nice chat?" he asked sarcastically. "Because she practically bit my head off."

"I think she sounded better, Dad," Anna said, hoping her words would placate him.

He stuffed the phone into a pocket. "Quite a temper on that girl."

"According to Mom, she got it from you."

"Maybe she did, maybe she did." He puffed out some air. "You want to go to L.A. Farm for dinner? They've got the best ahi on the west side."

"I've got a date. Kind of." She rose. "I'd better do my homework and get ready."

Her father frowned but walked her out of the kitchen. "Not with the schmuck from New Year's Eve, I hope."

"Definitely not."

"Well, if he hurts you—whoever he is—let me know. I'll kick his ass."

"I'll pass on the message." Anna smiled. At least her dad was taking interest, albeit in a Neanderthal kind of way. Maybe it was true. Maybe he *was* making progress. And maybe Anna could take some of the credit for his change. Maybe by standing her ground, she was finally teaching people to treat her the way she deserved to be treated.

Maybe this whole L.A. experiment was beginning to work.

Big Al's

Don't blow it, Adam told himself for perhaps the six zillionth time in the last forty-five minutes. He of the "Ben Stiller good looks" was feeling pretty fine with his new buzz cut and the way it showed off the tiny blue star tattoo behind his left ear. His good sense of humor and low-key style had its own unique appeal with the ladies, and his point-guard physique was becoming more sculpted each day. Adam Flood flew on everyone's radar. There wasn't an unkind word to be said about him. But still, Anna Percy was like no other girl Adam had ever encountered.

When he'd met her at the Friends of Sam Sharpe table at Jackson Sharpe's wedding, he'd been knocked out by her fresh, natural beauty. Who wouldn't have been? Sure, she'd come with Ben Birnbaum. But during the course of the evening he and Anna had spent enough time talking for Adam to realize that Ben was one lucky guy. Always had been, always would be.

Adam smiled. What a difference three days could make. Now he was on his way to pick up Anna, and

Ben Birnbaum was nowhere in sight. Even better, Anna had told him that she had no romantic interest in Ben at all. Adam had a hard time believing that—he'd seen how Anna had gazed at Ben at the wedding. But still, facts were facts. He was about to spend the evening with her, and Ben was out of the picture.

Driving his mom's Saturn, he picked Anna up at her father's house—she still managed to look regal in old Levi's, sneakers, and a Trinity sweatshirt—and then fought the late afternoon traffic on Sunset Boulevard, through Santa Monica and the mountainous Pacific Palisades, out to where it merged into the Pacific Coast Highway. A drive up the PCH was an event in itself. Set off a cliff lining the edge of the gorgeous white beach, melting into the endless blue ocean, with the bright yellow sun beating against the cloudless sky, there was nothing quite like it.

Adam pulled into Gladstone's parking lot. They bypassed the shivering tourists with their drinks on the boardwalk-size deck and led Bowser down to the flood-lit beach. Together they stood in the sand, looking at the ocean as Bowser ran happy circles around them. And now that Adam was ordering him back in the car, he was showing an unusual amount of resistance.

"Down, Bowser!" Adam instructed as the king-size mutt ran in excited circles around Anna, periodically jumping up to lick at her face. "He seems to have turned selectively deaf. But I think he's in love with you."

"Yes, I love you too, Bowser," she said, backing away from the dog. "Now, *sit!*"

The dog sat.

"Impressive," Adam admitted. "Maybe you'd better be the one to tell him to get in the car."

She did. Bowser obeyed instantly, sprawling across the backseat and staring up at Anna with pure love in his eyes.

"Maybe you need to be his full-time trainer," Adam told Anna.

"I suspect that your Bowser is a bit of a con artist. I'd check the bathroom mirror for paw prints if I were you."

Adam grinned. Was this girl great or what? "Hey, you hungry?"

"Yes, actually."

"There's a little burger shack up toward Malibu where we can eat out on a patio overlooking the ocean." He motioned to the throng at Gladstone's that was spilling into the parking lot. "I promise, no tourists."

"That sounds great." Anna looked down at the dog. "You want a burger, don't you, Bowser?"

Twenty minutes later, after a reasonably swift drive up the Pacific Coast Highway, Adam turned the Saturn into a small parking lot. "This is it," he announced, pointing at the A-frame structure. "Big Al's."

Anna peered at the carved wooden sign on the door. "It says Tofu Shack."

Adam groaned. "Tofu Shack? This is Big Al's! He

was an old biker who wouldn't go within a football field of tofu. All meat, all the time."

"When was the last time you were here?"

"Summer," Adam admitted.

"Well, either Big Al had a spiritual epiphany or he sold the place."

"Tofu," Adam muttered disgustedly. "Edible cardboard. But if you like it, we could—"

"Why don't we just get something to drink?" Anna suggested. "You said there's a patio, and I'm sure it's beautiful. It's already pretty late."

"Works for me. And let's bring the dog. If they say anything, I'll tell them we're on the board of PETA."

But the Tofu Shack had no problems with Bowser so long as he stayed under their table. The aging hippie waitress even brought him a bowl of cold water. Ten minutes later the three of them—two humans and one mutt—were sitting contentedly with their drinks two hundred feet above the Pacific, the waves below them crashing against the beachfront. Offshore, the lights of a few passing boats bobbed gently in the night.

Anna inhaled deeply. "Mmmm. I love that sea smell."

"Me too. One of my many life goals is to live on the ocean. Of course, around here, you have to be mighty rich to pull that one off."

"Is that one of your life goals, too?" Anna asked. "To get mighty rich?"

"Not really. It's kind of like a sickness in Beverly Hills. 'I'm rich, therefore I am' or something."

"Life is easier with money, though," Anna said softly.

"Yeah, but . . . I don't know. Maybe it's overrated. I'm thinking I'll buy some old heap of a sailboat, fix it up, and take it around the world or something."

"That sounds great."

He looked surprised. "Are you serious?"

"Why wouldn't I be?"

"Most of the girls in Beverly Hills are only interested in yachts. Preferably over a hundred feet, with a service staff of twenty."

"My mother belongs to a club on Long Island that has several vessels that could float the White House," she said. "I've been on a couple. It's hardly a great adventure."

"Is that what you're looking for? Adventure?"

Bowser put his snout on Anna's foot; she reached down to stroke his head. "I suppose I am. That's one of the reasons I left New York."

"Beverly Hills is not exactly a jungle safari."

"I don't know about that," Anna said.

He laughed. "Yeah, I guess it can be rugged."

"There's just so much jockeying for position here, so much emphasis on superficial things. God, now, that's a cliché judgment if there ever was—"

"No, I know what you mean. But you can't take that crap seriously. Who got wasted at whose party? Whose outfit is most expensive? Who got the biggest implants? Who cares?"

"Exactly," Anna agreed. "Anyway, next year we'll both go off to college, and this'll all seem like a bad dream."

"Do you know where you're going?"

"Yale. You?"

"This buddy of mine teaches at a sports academy in inner-city Detroit. I've been thinking about going back to Michigan for a year to help out."

"A year off? I never even considered that," Anna mused, considering it now and liking what she was thinking.

"Don't tell my parents. They may look like liberals, but when I mentioned the idea, I thought they were both going to spontaneously combust at the dinner table."

Anna laughed. Once again Adam nearly had to pinch himself. Sure, he'd had girlfriends before. But none of them had been like this girl. With tendrils of wheat-colored hair blowing against her cheeks from the breeze and her eyes sparkling in the moonlight, she looked so . . . alive. So genuine. So like the girl he'd always dreamed of but was sure he could never have.

Don't get ahead of yourself, he told himself. *Maybe she only thinks of you as a friend. Which is the kiss of death.*

Her left hand was near his right one. He could take it so easily. No big deal. All he had to do was—

At that moment Anna moved her hand away.

Damn.

"It's nice out here," she said.

"Yeah."

Just friends, he told himself, disappointed. *Once again with a girl I really like, it's going to be "just friends."*

Which was why he was so surprised when she leaned over and kissed him.

Bloated, Painted Clown

O kay, dreams don't necessarily mean squat.

That's what Sam told herself the next morning as she showered, letting the scalding hot water blast down on her shoulders. Jeez, what a dream. It starred her and Anna. And it was a replay of a real-life moment from Dee's sweet sixteen party, when Dee's parents had rented the Dorothy Chandler Pavilion—the same concert hall where they used to hold the Oscars—for the party. They'd hired a set designer to convert the place into a Vegas casino, complete with showgirls and live animals.

In real life, someone had slipped some high-test Russian vodka into the punch, and Sam had gotten totally wasted. Just to be outrageous, she had kissed Dee in the middle of the stage. To her surprise, she'd kind of liked it.

In Sam's dream it had been her own sweet sixteen. For a goof the party had an Oscar theme—she'd just received the fictitious Academy Award for best director. Anna had been the presenter. When Anna had handed her the gold statuette, she'd kissed her. Not on the cheek, either. But on the lips.

And . . . Sam had kissed her back. Like *really* kissed her back, as the theme from *Titanic* had swelled in the background.

Very weird. Because she was certain she wasn't gay. The lust bunny had jumped into her boy-cut La Perla silk panties many a time for many a guy. She wasn't as slutty as, say, Cammie Sheppard—who *was?*—but she'd had her share of hookups. So what was up with the dream, then?

Maybe it was because Anna had been with Ben, and Sam had crushed on Ben for so long? Some kind of bizarre brain-wave syntax-firing blip?

It couldn't *possibly* be because she was gay. No flippin' way.

"Hey, wait up," Sam called to Anna, who she saw walking toward the high school building. It was another beautiful, sunny L.A. morning. Sam hurried to catch up as quickly as her stiletto heels would permit.

It was three hours later. When she'd dressed, she'd taken a last appraising look at herself in her three-way, floor-length mirror. She loved the Asian-inspired red-and-violet-silk Yohji Yamamoto fitted T-shirt, the cropped red leather Valentino jacket, and the size-eight Gucci jeans, which were surprisingly slimming, considering how low cut they were. Just before breakfast the family limo had arrived with her hair guy, Raymond, so he could do a blowout at home. (Sam couldn't imagine sitting with the other I'm-getting-a-blowout-before-I-start-my-day types at his brand-new salon, Menage.) As usual, Raymond had done a spectacular job; with the help of his new Raymond's Genius hair extensions, her hair looked thick and luxurious.

But even with all that, plus makeup applied the way she'd learned at Valerie's cosmetics emporium, Anna Percy—who wore nothing more elaborate than a long-sleeved black T-shirt, low-slung black pants, and utterly non-trendy Capezio dance flats—made Sam feel like a bloated, painted clown.

"Hi, Sam. What's up?"

"The party-at-my-place-and-film-it thing is out for this weekend," Sam told Anna as they entered the building together. "Listen, how many synonyms do you know for stupid?"

Anna looked confused. "Sorry?"

"Dumb, dull, retarded, thick, moronic, dim-witted, imbecilic, pea brained," Sam answered herself as they cut through the building and out onto the quad. "They all apply to my new—gag me—stepmom, who has decided to redo my home in her image, beginning this weekend. Ergo, no party."

"Can't we just shoot it in a club?" Anna suggested. "Someplace decadent?"

"Been there, done that," Sam replied. "A guy last year did a short film at Au Bar that made it into the L.A. Film Festival. We need something fresh. We really

need to get it together by this weekend if we want to—
wait. I've got it. Veronique's Maison!"

"Veronica's house?" Anna translated.

"It's this incredible spa in Palm Springs," Sam
explained. "I was thinking of going up there later in the
month anyway. Here, check it out. Look in the very back."
She pulled the latest edition of *Los Angeles* magazine out
of her backpack and handed it to Anna, who flipped to the
last page, where she found the tiniest of boxed ads.

It read simply: *VERONIQUE'S MAISON. 2006 waiting
list only. E-mail only to reserve@veronique-palmsprings.com.
NO calls.*

"2006? Impressive," Anna said.

"They don't really need the ad; they only place it to
be snotty. Like, they don't even tell you it's a spa; you
just have to know. Trust me, this place is as Daisy
Buchanan as you can get. Mixed with a little Deepak
Chopra, but whatever. I think we should go this weekend. And film there."

Anna handed the magazine back to Sam. "I suppose
the waiting list doesn't apply to you."

"Your point?" Sam asked.

"None. But I really don't know if I can spend the
weekend away."

"Why not?"

"I might have plans."

"Change them."

"Adam and I were talking about going to the San
Diego Zoo."

"Yeah, I saw you two together yesterday." Sam worked hard not to look at Anna's mouth. Which was just so sick! The only reason she was even thinking about that was because of her stupid dream, which didn't mean anything. "Invite him to come out to V's. So, you and Adam, huh?"

Anna shrugged. "We're friends."

"Friends who get naked and do the nasty or the boring kind?"

Anna laughed. "I don't know yet."

Sam shook her perfectly streaked locks off her face. "Come on. You know if the vibe is there."

Anna looked contemplative. "Well, I kissed him last night."

Sam checked in with herself on how she felt about that, but everything was too jumbled together in her mind. She shrugged. "A kiss is just a kiss."

"*Casablanca.*" Anna smiled.

"Wait, I thought you told me you never went to the movies," Sam reminded her.

"Come on. *Casablanca* is a classic."

"And you're a classics kind of babe," Sam surmised. Oh God, did she sound *flirtatious?* Because that would be horrible! "So, anyway, how was it?"

"Nice."

"Translation—no chemistry," Sam surmised.

"It was a first kiss, not a scorched-earth policy."

"Chemistry is chemistry," Sam insisted. "Either you want to jump his bones or you don't. Hold on, I've got a phone call to make."

Sam pulled her cell from her purse and made a quick call to her father's executive assistant, telling her to book two suites at V's for the weekend.

"Done." Sam dropped the palm-size phone back into her purse with a big smile. "We'll have a blast." Her gut told her that the Anna and Adam thing wasn't exactly torrid. Plus the thought of spending the weekend at a spa with Anna made her feel . . . happy. "And it's on me," she added.

"That's not necessary, but thanks for the offer. Listen, if we're going to do a film, won't we need to write a script?" Anna pointed out.

Sam shook her head. "We'll just improv and see what we get."

"I think that's another way of saying we'll be unprepared."

Sam sighed. Why was Anna being difficult? "Fine, I'll write a—"

"Why don't I do it?" Anna interrupted. "You're directing and producing, the least I can do is write."

Sam was dubious. "Have you ever written a screenplay?"

"No. But we're only talking about, what, a ten-minute film? Everyone has to start somewhere."

"Really, Anna, I should—"

"No, *I* should," Anna insisted. "It's a co-project, remember?"

"*Fine*," Sam acquiesced, though she was not happy about it. She checked her new Cartier Tank watch.

"Damn, I'm late to meet Cammie. Listen, meet me after school at the Beverly Hills Hotel and we can plan the whole thing."

"Why the Beverly Hi—"

"Convenient, cool, beats Starbucks. Gotta run. Catch you later."

Sam took off, her mind buzzing. She was used to giving directions, not taking them. On the other hand, she kind of liked that Anna Percy was no pushover. One could say, Sam found it very . . . attractive.

Screw Hazelden

"Hi, Sam," the Angelina Jolie look-alike waitress said as she reached behind her head and pulled a pen out of her ponytail.

"The usual?"

"Yeah. Thanks, Madeline. Anna?"

"Espresso would be great," Anna said.

The girls were seated in the Polo Lounge, the outdoor café at the Beverly Hills Hotel. Surrounded by a spectacular array of palm trees and flowers in brilliant shades of pink and rose, Anna was reminded of the afternoon teas she'd once had there with her grandparents when she was little.

Though it was early January, all Anna needed to wear over her T-shirt was a denim jacket. Sam leaned her elbows on the table. One of her hands came to rest atop Anna's. "So, I've been thinking about how perfect it is for us to do this project together. It's like you're Daisy and I'm Jay."

Anna tried to figure out what Sam could possibly mean by that remark. In *The Great Gatsby*, Jay Gatsby had a massive crush on the wealthy Daisy Buchanan. He became wealthy himself. But somehow his "new" money wasn't considered as good as her "old" money. Though Jay did everything he could, he never quite convinced Daisy—or himself—that he was good enough for her.

What was Sam implying? Was it about money? Class? Or something else?

No. It couldn't be romance. Sam was straight.

But. Just in case. Anna dead-eyed Sam's hand over her own. "Care to explain?" she asked, casually withdrawing her hand.

"Just kidding. I'm thinking when we get to V's, we should suss out the social-climbing nouveau faction and ask them if they want to be in a movie. People always say yes, especially when they realize who I am."

"What if they can't act?" Anna asked. "Someone has to do the dialogue that I'm going to write."

Sam waved dismissively. "Think of the guests as wallpaper. We'll definitely have your basic filthy-rich snooty types from back east. You might even know some of them. Any luck, some filthy-rich guy who made his money in Internet porn will be visiting from Texas. That'll add some, ahem, color. Cut and paste, mix and match, splice them in around the script, and voilà: we've got a visual commentary on the modern American aristocracy that would make F. Scott proud. So, what about your script?"

"What about it?" Anna said, hoping she sounded confident.

"You've thought about it?"

"Sure," Anna improvised. That was true. She *had* thought about it. She just hadn't come to any conclusions.

"Main characters, at least?" Sam prompted.

"A Gatsby type, of course. And . . . a Daisy type. And probably another girl." Anna was making it up as she went along. "Maybe Parker Pinelli could play Gatsby?" She'd met Parker at the wedding, too. He was a stunningly handsome BHH senior who allegedly was an actor.

"Why, are you interested in Parker now?" Sam asked.

Anna noticed a sharpness to Sam's tone. "Not at all. But he can act, right?"

"Using the term loosely," Sam allowed. "Yeah, he'll do in a heartbeat. We'll get his brother, Monty, to help out, too. I'll give some thought to the Daisy character and get back to you. Unless you want to be Daisy."

"*Definitely* not. And there's only one other casting absolute: No Cammie Sheppard."

"You have my word," Sam said with a chuckle. Anna wasn't sure what the chuckle was meant to imply. And she didn't really care, quite frankly. If Anna's low opinion of Cammie Sheppard was comical to Sam, so be it. As long as Cammie stayed far away from the set.

"Here you go, Sam." The waitress set a cup of coffee and an iced crystal goblet of fresh raspberries in front of her. "Hey, I got a callback for your dad's new film."

"Good for you," Sam said.

"It's just one scene—I'd be a go-go dancer at the Limelight who has information your dad's character needs to find his kidnapped lover. But it's killer."

"Great, Madeline. Hope you get it."

Madeline held up crossed fingers, then went on to the next table. Sam tore open a packet of Equal and shook it into her coffee. "I swear, everyone in this town is delusional. I've seen her reel. She sucks."

"Why doesn't someone tell her the truth, then?"

"You're in La La Land now, Anna. The truth is always relative." Sam plucked a raspberry from her goblet with French-manicured fingers and popped it into her mouth. "Lots of girls who can't act make it. If she makes it, you don't want to be the one who dissed her. Or she could be sleeping with someone really important. You dis her, she tells him . . . *or her* . . . you're screwed. And other variations on that theme." Sam chewed another raspberry, then lowered her voice. "They use girls like her for the 'box' scene."

"Which is . . . ?" Anna asked.

"You know how there's always a still photo of a babe in a bikini or her underwear on the box of every DVD movie? It's supposed to attract buyers and renters to the film, even if it has nothing to do with the picture. Want one?" She pushed the berries toward Anna.

"No thanks. Actually, I think I'll head back to my dad's and start writing. Any ideas for a plot?"

"Pound away, we'll see what you come up with," Sam

said, sipping her coffee. "But don't go yet. Let's hang out awhile."

Unfortunately, Anna really was itching to start writing. She'd been accused many a time of living with her nose in a book but had never thought about actually becoming a writer. Maybe it would turn out that she had talent. That is, if she could come up with an actual story for their film. "I read somewhere that Fitzgerald came out here to be a screenwriter," she recalled.

"And failed miserably," Sam added. "It only *seemed* easy."

"Well, then I really better get started," Anna said as she rose to gather her things. Progress was definitely being made. A few days ago she would have felt guilty leaving Sam alone. But Sam could fend for herself.

And so could Anna.

A half hour later, when Anna pulled her car into the circular driveway, there was a red Saleen Mustang parked close to the front walkway. Her first thought was: *Ben.* Her second thought was to tell her first thought to shut up.

First, she knew Ben drove a Maserati. Second, just because he'd sent her balloons the day before didn't mean he'd try to stand in for those balloons today. Third, Anna knew he had to get back to New Jersey for the start of classes at Princeton. Chances were good he was already there. But even if by some fluke he was still in town and it was his car, that did not mean—fourth— that she would talk to him.

"Anna?" The car door opened. It wasn't Ben. It was her sister.

"*Susan?*"

"Got a hug for your big sis?" Susan came over to her with outstretched arms.

Anna got out of her Lexus and embraced her sister, all the while wondering how this could be. She'd spoken to Susan at Hazelden twenty-four hours before. She knew her older sister wasn't due to leave the rehab facility for several more weeks.

Susan hugged her back hard. "I missed you so much!"

"I missed you, too," Anna said. "But what are you doing here?"

"Hey, you're supposed to be glad to see me." Susan flipped her platinum-blond hair off her face. She was a half inch shorter than Anna, and an impartial observer would have said not quite as classically beautiful. But when Susan was at the top of her game, Anna knew that her sister could be stunning—though now in a downtown, rebel kind of way. At the moment she was a little on the plump side with an edgy, sexy look: lots of smudgy black eyeliner, red lipstick, tight jeans, and a sleeveless white muscle T-shirt under a black leather motorcycle jacket. Her hair was naturally the same color as Anna's, but for the past couple of years she'd been bleaching it Courtney Love white blond. It drove their mom insane, which Susan took as an excellent reason to keep doing it.

"I *am* glad to see you," Anna said, stepping back

from her sister and giving her an appraising look. "You look great. I mean it, too."

Susan shook her head. "No, I don't. I'm a blob. I need to drop fifteen in a hurry. Flipping rehab mac and cheese and endless Snickers bars. Hey, every addict needs something."

Anna looped an arm through hers. "Well . . . just come on inside. Why were you out here, anyway?"

Susan squeezed her arm. "Because I really don't want to see Dad, that's why. I was waiting for you. Hey, how do you like my ride?" She patted the top of the red Saleen. "Pretty hot, huh? Zero to sixty in three point three."

"Yeah, great," Anna said distractedly. "So. Here you are. In Los Angeles."

Susan reached into her pocket for cigarettes. "Gee. Don't hyperventilate with happiness or anything."

"It's just . . . you weren't due to get out of Hazelden for—"

"Screw Hazelden," Susan said, torching her cigarette and taking a deep drag. "Because of Hazelden, I'm smoking again and I'm fat. So I checked myself out." She made a pouty face at her sister. "Oh, come on, Anna. Lighten up. I'm fine. Really. I was worried about you, all alone here with dear old Dad. It's not like he's going to look out for you or anything."

Anna was tempted to say that Susan had never looked out for Anna, either; in fact, it had been Anna who'd always been the one to look out for Susan. Susan needed looking after. Anna didn't. But no one ever talked about it. That was just the way their family worked.

"Dad's trying to change," Anna said instead as she opened the door.

"Thrilling." Susan chucked her burning Marlboro Light into the shrubbery. "I'm not staying here, no matter what. He's not home now, is he?"

"Doubtful."

"Then I'll come in." They stepped into the foyer, and Susan took in the spacious surroundings. "My entire apartment in the East Village could fit in this hallway."

"You don't have to live in a dive, you know," Anna reminded her. "So, where do you plan to stay?"

"Maybe I'll get a bungalow at the Beverly Hills Hotel. Remember when we got a bungalow there for the opening of the Getty Center art museum? It was so great."

"That's funny. I was there this afternoon. The hotel, I mean. I was meeting with someone about a school project. But look, Sooz, Dad's got tons of room—"

"Forget it. Just show me to the bathroom, then we're on our way."

"Come up to my room with me. I want to chuck my jacket," Anna said. Her sister's face darkened. "Don't worry. He's definitely not home. You won't see him."

Reluctantly Susan followed Anna upstairs. As soon as they reached the hallway, they were hit with an overpowering smell of roses. The closer they got to her room, the stronger the scent became. "Jeez, you think the maid used enough air freshener?" Susan asked.

Anna opened her door. "Holy shit," Susan breathed.

Every horizontal surface of Anna's room was covered in roses: crimson and cherry red, pale and dusky pink, white, yellow, even orange. Some were in vases, some were strewn across on her bed, and some blanketed the carpets and hardwood floor.

There was a note in the center of the bed.

ANNA—
  I'M STILL IN TOWN. LET ME MAKE IT
UP TO YOU. CALL ME. PLEASE.
                                   —BEN

Susan read the card over Anna's shoulder. "Ben who?"

"A guy I met on the flight from New York." Anna crumpled up the note and threw it toward her trash basket. Why was Ben making it so difficult for her to do the right thing? If he really cared about her, he'd let her go . . . wouldn't he?

"A guy who sent you like a thousand roses—"

"That I'm about to have removed by one of the maids." With studied nonchalance, Anna went to her closet—crushing rose petals all the way—and hung up the jacket.

"What does he mean, 'let me make it up to you'?" Susan asked as she brushed rose petals from Anna's bed so she could plop down on it.

"It doesn't matter. He's a bastard."

Susan smiled knowingly. "A hot bastard?"

"Very," Anna admitted. "But there's more to life than that."

"Honey, I've been locked up for three weeks with about a hundred Twelve Steppers in training. Right now, I can't think of anything better than a hot bastard."

"Not this one. Trust me. Come on, let's go."

"Let's take my car," Susan said. "I never get to drive in Manhattan."

Downstairs, Anna found the cook and gave her thirty dollars to take the roses to the closest battered-women's shelter. Then they went out to Susan's car. They were just pulling out of the driveway when Django turned in. The dark roots of his platinum-bleached hair were showing more and more each day.

"Whoa, who the hell was that?" Susan asked, craning to get another glimpse.

"Dad's driver. He lives in the guest house."

"He's renting it?"

"I think it's part of his salary."

"Buttoned-up Dad hired a guy who wears rings? On his thumbs?"

"Dad's pretty unbuttoned these days," Anna replied. "Turn left, you'll head toward Sunset Boulevard. So, how long are you planning to stay?"

Susan followed her sister's directions. "I'm playing it by ear. Anyway, let's do something fun this weekend, okay?"

"Can't. I'm writing a short film and going to a spa in Palm Springs to film it."

"Since when do *you* write films?"

"Since now, I guess."

"Anna, you don't even go to the movies. Now, if it was a novel—"

"This is for school," Anna explained. "And I go to the movies."

"Yeah, if there are subtitles."

Anna smiled. She was used to Susan's ribbing, and she'd missed it. She'd missed *her*. "You should come to the spa with me. It'll be fun."

"How do you know?" Susan's voice was skeptical.

"I have a feeling Sam Sharpe doesn't do boring."

"Girl Sam or boy Sam?"

"Girl Sam. Jackson Sharpe's daughter."

"Cool. I *love* Jackson Sharpe."

"So come. Sam says this spa is incredible. Wouldn't you like a little first-class pampering?"

"Yeah, actually I would. At Hazelden we had to scrub each other's toilets. My roommate made Ilsa, She-Wolf of the Nazi SS, look like a pussycat. While I was cleaning, she stood over me with a flipping checklist."

Anna was incredulous. "You cleaned toilets?"

"*Toilet*," Susan corrected. "After the first time, I paid someone else to do it. I mean, come on. I've got an eight-digit trust fund. How ludicrous is it to make me pretend to be humble?"

"I don't know. You live in the East Village and pretend to be poor," Anna pointed out.

"Poor little rich girl, slumming it. I'm a cliché," Susan admitted.

"I still don't understand why you live down there."

"Hey, I'm the only girl on Avenue D who has a cleaning lady." They came to another light, and a silver Porsche Carrera pulled up alongside them. Susan looked over at the driver—a guy in his fifties—and revved the Mustang's engine. The guy grinned, and Susan winked at him. Anna remembered when her older sister had followed the rules of propriety even better than she had. But that felt like a long, long time ago.

"I like the people who live downtown more than I like the people in our old stomping grounds," Susan said. "The air is just too-too on the Upper East Side. Besides, I love to make Mom apoplectic."

Which Anna already knew. It just seemed like Susan should be getting over it already. But she didn't say anything as the light changed and Susan hit the gas pedal. "Follow that Bronco, the one turning right onto Beverly Drive. You make the right and then a quick left into the Beverly Hills Hotel drive."

Susan made the same right turn as the Bronco, and a moment later they were passing the green-and-white sign welcoming visitors to the hotel. "Nice. I won't be missing my squalor at all."

Susan stopped the car at the entrance. The same

valet who'd greeted Anna earlier opened the doors. "Welcome back, miss," he said to Anna.

"Thank you. My sister will be checking in. Her bags are in the back."

"Very good. Just go inside and register; I'll take care of these."

Anna pressed a few dollars into his hand and then went inside with Susan.

"So here's the plan, little sister," Susan said as they joined a short line at the registration desk. The hotel lobby was cavernous. Done in shades of pale pink and gray, with pale pink leather club chairs dotting the entire area, the whole expanse of it was shaded by giant potted palms.

"I brought two string bikinis and one of 'em has your name on it. Let's go get changed, then sit by the pool and count how many guys try to hit on us."

A Private Screening

Dee and Cammie hung out at the Beverly Hills Hotel the way other kids hung out at the mall. In fact, it just so happened that as Susan was checking into the hotel, they were fixing their makeup in the ladies' room just off the lobby. This was after spending the previous hour flirting with some guys at the bar in the Polo Lounge. Allegedly these guys were musicians, in town because their band was opening for Avril Lavigne at the Pond in Anaheim the next night.

A quarter hour earlier the guys had invited Cammie and Dee to go club hopping. Dee had been ready to go, but Cammie wasn't so high on the idea. The guys had only rated a five on her basic one-to-ten scale, losing three points for opening for Avril but gaining a bonus point for their British accents. Dee had followed Cammie's lead in holding off from any firm response. Instead the girls had excused themselves to the restroom.

As they stood in front of the mirrored vanity, Dee watched Cammie admire her own reflection. She wore a washed-pink La Perla silk camisole under a cropped pink Gucci jacket, with jeans cut so low you could see her hip bones and even a hint of where those hip bones led. The strappy pink-and-white polka-dot open-toed pumps she'd special ordered from Christian Louboutin made her legs seem to go on forever. She had a perfect French manicure on her toenails and a Harry Winston gold-and-diamond ankle bracelet on her left ankle. As usual, her wild red-gold tendrils curled over one eye and halfway down her back.

It was an accepted fact that Cammie knew she was gorgeous. In fact, she often said, if she ever had an inclination toward girls, the person she'd want to do was herself.

Cammie retouched her lip gloss, and Dee instantly looked at her own lips. Thinner. Smaller. She sighed. It was impossible to be with Cammie and not be spell-bound by her self-confidence.

Not that looks are the most important thing, Dee mentally added. *The flesh is fleeting, the body a mere vessel. Still, at least I'm better-looking than Sam.*

"So, do you want to go out with those guys?" Dee asked.

Cammie sprayed herself with Très Cammie, a made-to-order perfume her father had commissioned for her sixteenth birthday. "That's like asking if we want to be bored to death."

"I wish you'd said that before. We could have made the six o'clock spinning class at Yoga Booty."

"Spinning is for fools. We live in Los Angeles, where

you can ride seventeen miles right on the beach from Santa Monica to Palos Verdes. Who'd want to sit on a stationary bike in a gym and pedal to nowhere?"

Dee sighed. Sometimes it was hard to be Cammie's best friend because Cammie had so many hostility issues. These last few days, especially, had been difficult. They'd seen Ben at the wedding with that new girl, Anna. Cammie had made a play to try to get him back. And Ben had turned her down.

"You know, you were much nicer when you and Ben were a couple."

Cammie dropped the tiny perfume bottle back into her Chanel clutch. "And?"

"*And* I think you compare every guy you meet to him."

"In his dreams." Cammie snorted.

"Ben's awesome. I know how happy you were with him, and I know how much you want him back. I'm really sorry it's not all going according to plan." This was the very first time in Dee's memory that Cammie had not reeled in a boy she wanted. It was all because of Anna Percy. She had to give Anna props for that. Ben was a great guy. The happiest that Dee ever had seen Cammie was when she and Ben were a couple. Ben had made Cammie . . . kinder. Not kind, but kinder.

That wasn't to say that Dee thought Ben was right for Anna. He was so much more right for, say, *her*. She and Ben had shared that one magical night together in Princeton a couple of months ago on Dee's East Coast

college tour. He'd been a little wasted. Maybe even a *lot*
wasted. But so what? It had still been magical.

Cammie didn't even know the Dee-Ben interlude
had ever occurred. Neither did Sam. Dee knew better
than to tell either of her best friends anything truly
important. But she'd mentioned it to Anna on New
Year's Day, after deciding that in her own pursuit of
Ben Birnbaum, the best defense was a good offense.

Cammie shook her curls off her face. "I could get
Ben back if I really wanted to."

"Acceptance is the first step toward healing, Cammie."

"Dee, please don't go all New Age on me. I'm so not
in the mood." Cammie headed back to the Polo Lounge
with Dee in her wake. "What I think we should do is—
wait a minute."

"For what?" Dee asked, confused.

Cammie nodded toward the hotel front desk, where
someone had just caught her eye. Someone lithe, blond,
and effortlessly lovely. "Look at that. Well, well, well."

"Anna Percy."

"Yep." Cammie's venom toward Anna was palpable.
Cammie wanted Ben; Anna had Ben. It was that simple.
Cammie had simply never lost at love before.

"Why would Anna be checking in?" Dee wondered.

Cammie's cat eyes gleamed and a smile curled on her
lips. "Maybe there's more to Little Miss East Coast Preppie
than meets the eye."

"Who do you think she's with?" Dee whispered.

"Maybe it's her girlfriend."

Dee would never have guessed. "You think?"

"You never know," Cammie said, chuckling.

Dee wasn't sure if Cammie was serious or joking.

Before Dee could probe, Cammie was already walking across the lobby directly toward Anna and the mystery girl. Dee had no choice but to follow her.

"Anna!" Cammie said gaily. "How great to run into you!"

"Hi, Anna!" Dee chimed in, throwing her diminutive arms around Anna's neck. "This is so cool! Gee, what are you doing here?"

Anna's reaction to Cammie was impassive. So much so, Dee couldn't tell what Anna was feeling at all. But she was sure of one thing—it definitely wasn't joy.

"Hello, Cammie. Dee."

"Who's your friend?" Cammie asked slyly.

"This is my sister, Susan," Anna said. "Susan, Cammie Sheppard and Delia Young. We go to school together."

Dee knew it! No way was Anna a lesbian. Her energy was one hundred percent heterosexual.

"Poor you, school sucks," Susan said cheerfully.

"Miss Percy? Here are the keys to your bungalow." The handsome man behind the front desk handed Susan an envelope. "Will you be needing another set?"

"Yes," Susan said. "My sister's staying with me."

"No, I'm not," Anna objected, her voice low.

"Yeah, you are," Susan said, and the desk clerk instantly handed her a second envelope, which she slapped into Anna's palm. "So, we were just about to slip into bikinis, hang by the pool, and see who makes us drool. Care to join us?"

"You know, that is such a great idea!" Cammie said.

"Um, Cammie?" Dee began, wondering why in the world Cammie would want to spend part of the evening with a girl she despised. "Those guys are waiting for us—"

"Forget them. I'd much rather hang out with Anna and Susan." Cammie flashed her most charming smile at Susan. "Just give us a minute. Dee and I will go downstairs to the Promenade—they've got some decent shops down there, and we'll get some cute bikinis. Then we'll meet you at the pool, okay?"

"Great," Susan said. "Whichever one of us gets hit on the least buys dinner."

Cammie laughed. "Anna, I really like your sister. This will be fun—a chance to get to know each other better. So, we'll see you in a little bit."

"Catch." Susan tossed the two tiny pieces of a crocheted tangerine-colored bikini across the bungalow's bedroom. They fell at Anna's feet. "I can't wear this one until I lose some weight. I swear, you could snort lines off my ass. But it'll look great on you. For which I hate you, by the by."

Anna sat on the edge of the four-poster mahogany bed, making no effort to retrieve the bikini. "Susan, listen. I really have no desire to hang out with those girls. I don't like them. Neither will you."

Susan was pawing through one of her valises. "Why not?"

"They're awful, that's why."

"Aha!" Susan extracted a more conservative black Anika Brazil halter two-piece and held it aloft triumphantly.

"Seriously, Sooz," Anna went on. "They're superficial. And bitchy."

"Sounds like half the people we grew up with," Susan said as she stepped out of her Seven jeans.

"That's not true and you know it."

"Oh, come on. I mean, I realize a girl as perfect as you are has very high standards, but lighten up a little. We're hanging out at the pool, not getting married."

"It's just that I worry about you, Sooz," Anna said. "There's a bar there."

"I keep telling you, I'm fine. Clean and sober, walking the straight and narrow, Your Honor."

"But if rehab helps you . . ."

"Hey, I'm Jane Percy's daughter," Susan said lightly. "I can help myself." She gave Anna a quick hug. "Come on. Don't be mad. You're one of the only people in this whole messed-up world who I love, Anna."

"Ditto," Anna said, hugging her sister back.

"Okay, then. Enough with the love fest." Susan slipped into the halter. "Fortunately any weight I put on above the waist went to my tits. How does this look? Great, right?"

Susan did look pretty fantastic. Too fantastic to be sequestered away from the pool by an overprotective little sister.

By the time Anna and Susan reached the pool, a crescent moon had risen high above the hotel, and a downy blanket of steam covered the heated pool itself. They found four unoccupied chaise longues—they had their pick, as the well-lit pool area was largely deserted except for the outdoor bar/restaurant against the far wall. Instantly a waiter was at their side. "Good evening. Can I bring you ladies anything?"

"Rum and Coke," Susan ordered.

Anna paled.

"Kidding," Susan added quickly, rolling her eyes. "Hold the rum."

"A bottle of Evian, thanks," Anna told the waiter

"Now, this is more like it." Susan stretched out thankfully as the waiter went to retrieve their drinks. "No snow. No toilets to clean. No fat-ass therapist telling me how screwed up I am because of my family of origin but that it doesn't matter because I have an opportunity now to take charge of my life."

"Did he really say that?"

"He was a she, and hell, yes. It's such crapola. Oh my God, Anna, look over there." Susan nudged her chin toward the other side of the pool, where two good-looking guys chatted away on their cells. Plates of untouched sushi sat on a table between them.

"So?" Anna asked.

"What planet are you on? That's Alex Souter and Noah Monahan."

"Who are they?"

"Didn't you see the Oscars? They won a best screenplay award together. And Alex, the taller one with the dark hair, just starred in a big Christmas action movie—I forget the name. But he was smoking. Noah, the blond, is turning to producing."

It struck Anna as a significant accomplishment to have won an Academy Award for best screenplay. Not the level of a PEN/Faulkner Award for literature, but still. It would be interesting to be with a guy like that. Her best friend, Cyn, back in New York, would have already sauntered right over and introduced herself. Ten minutes later they'd probably have been making out in the Jacuzzi—all three of them.

I could be that girl, Anna thought. The word *audacious* came to mind. Yes. She could be audacious. In control and audacious.

The waiter was at the pool bar. Anna excused herself and went to him, explained what she wanted, then returned to her chaise longue.

Susan eyed her, eyebrows raised. "What did you just do?"

"I just sent—what are their names again?"

"Those guys? Alex Souter and Noah Monahan."

"Right." Anna stretched out on the chaise. "I just sent them drinks."

"Get out!" Susan said, laughing. "You did not.

You've never done anything remotely like that in your entire life."

"That," Anna said, "is exactly the point of my being out here."

Still, Anna's stomach fluttered as she waited for the drinks to be delivered. She was keeping her eyes on the two famous guys, she hoped without being obvious about it, when Cammie and Dee entered the pool area and walked right over to them. The guys halted their conversations to take in the sight of Cammie in her white Vix bikini. Its low-cut mesh top emphasized the perfect 34D breasts she'd purchased; the minute bottom was held together by strings. Dee sported an Anna Sui blue-and-yellow gingham bikini that showed off the results of hundreds of spinning classes and yoga sessions. To Anna and Susan's surprise, the guys put down their phones and started a conversation with Cammie and Dee.

Susan nudged Anna. "Your friends *know* those guys?"

"They're not my friends. And *we* had the secretary general of the UN to a dinner party in Mom's brownstone. I'd say that's quite a bit more impressive."

"I wouldn't," Susan said.

At that moment the waiter delivered Anna's drinks to Noah and Alex. He set the two tall glasses garnished with mint leaves in front of them, then cocked his chin toward Anna to show they were from her.

"What did you send them?" Susan asked.

"Iced tea."

"Long Island iced tea, I hope."

"The nonalcoholic kind," Anna admitted, blushing. Noah and Alex were looking over at her now. That part was fine. The problem was, so were Cammie and Dee. Cammie laughed and said something to Noah and Alex, which made them chuckle. The guys eyed Anna again and hoisted their drinks in a salute.

Smile, she told herself. *Smile flirtatiously. Because what the hell.*

Cammie and Dee headed for Anna and Susan, Alex and Noah in tow. Which was not exactly how Anna had envisioned this encounter turning out. But then, how could she have known that Cammie and Dee knew the two writers?

"Oh my God, Alex and Noah are heading over here," Susan hissed. She sucked in her stomach and tossed her hair over one eye. Anna didn't do anything at all except wait and feel slightly ridiculous.

"Well, well, you two look comfy," Cammie commented, stepping out of her strappy sandals. "We brought friends along."

"So I see." Susan smiled up at the famous guys. "Hi. I'm Susan."

"Hey. I'm Alex and this is Noah," Alex said, flashing the smile that apparently had sold millions of movie tickets. He sat on the edge of Cammie's chaise.

"We know," Susan said. "I loved your movie."

"Thanks." Noah's gaze went to Anna. "And thanks for the drinks."

"You're welcome," Anna replied. And couldn't think of another word to say.

"Do you have a name?" Alex added playfully, squatting down next to Anna's chaise.

"Yes. Right. Sorry." Anna sat up. "I'm Anna Percy." She extended her hand to shake his.

He seemed amused by her formality. "Did you like our movie, too, Anna Percy?"

"To tell you the truth, I didn't see it," Anna confessed.

Alex cracked up. "Trust you to find the one girl in America who didn't see it," Noah teased.

"So, how do you guys know each other?" Susan asked Cammie.

"My dad's their agent," Cammie said nonchalantly, stretching out on a chaise on the other side of Susan. "They were at our place for a barbecue the day after Christmas."

"Where was I?" Susan mock moaned.

"If you're around next time, I'll invite you," Cammie promised.

Susan beamed. "Great."

Noah put his fist to his heart, as if Anna had just wounded him. "You know how to hurt a guy."

"If I'd known I was going to meet you, I would have seen it," Anna explained.

She seemed to amuse him. "About a hundred million people saw it because they *wanted* to see it."

Anna reddened. "I don't go to the movies all that much."

"Gee, why not?" Dee asked.

"Most of them aren't very good," Anna said.

"Oh yeah, dig yourself in even deeper," Cammie hooted.

"Well, clearly I have to do something about this," Noah decided. He picked up the courtesy phone on the small table between the chaise longues. "Hi, this is Noah Monahan. . . . No, everything is fine, thanks. Listen, can you arrange to have *Piper's Dream* set up in my bungalow? Now would be great. Thanks. Ciao." He hung up and turned to Anna, wiggling his eyebrows in a Groucho Marx imitation while pretending to hold a cigar. "Come along, my dear. I've arranged a private screening."

Anna was momentarily flustered. "Um, I—"

He dropped the Groucho thing. "Hey, you're not really going to turn down a private screening of my movie, are you?"

Was she? And if she was, then why had she sent him drinks? It wasn't like she was in any danger. She was at the Beverly Hills Hotel, for God's sake. But what about Adam?

What about him? Anna thought. *I like him. A lot. But it's not like we're engaged.*

"Of course not," Anna agreed.

"Get down, sis," Susan exclaimed, egging her on.

Noah held out a hand and hoisted Anna to her feet. Standing, she was just slightly taller than he was. He had open blue eyes, tousled blond hair, and a toothy, boyish grin. She slipped her cover-up on over her bathing suit. Noah looked down at Anna's feet, clad in casual Chanel leather sandals. "Great sandals," he said.

Which was odd. Because they were actually rather ordinary, albeit extremely well made. She'd had them forever. But maybe he just wanted to find a unique way to compliment her, Anna figured.

"Thanks," she said.

"Okay, so let's go." He reached for her hand again.

Anna held back. "But how can they possibly find the movie and get it ready this quickly?"

He grinned at her. "Anna Percy, that's what they do here: make us happy."

"And now you're going to make each other happy," Cammie chimed, dripping insinuation.

Anna felt like making a public disclaimer: "No. I am not going to Noah Monahan's bungalow to have sex." But she forced herself to keep her mouth shut.

"Susan, I'll meet you back here in—" Anna looked over at Noah. "How long is it?

"An hour fifty-two. Unless they got the director's cut, which runs thirty minutes longer."

The notion of leaving Susan alone with Cammie did not fill Anna with confidence. But she couldn't very well hover over Susan like a bodyguard. Besides, she told herself, the Noah encounter was exactly the kind of thing she'd come to California for. Sort of.

"So you're okay?" she asked her sister.

Susan waved her off. "I'm fine."

"You two go bare your souls to each other," Cammie said with a grin. "I'll take really good care of your sister."

That's what Anna was afraid of.

Elegant Toes

The decor of Noah's bungalow was American Indian chic, with colorful Navajo rugs dotting the hardwood floor. Facing the big-screen TV was a plush sofa covered in copper, brown, and eggshell carved, totem-printed fabric. An ornate framed Indian headdress hung over it.

"Kick off your shoes, make yourself comfortable," Noah called as he headed into the kitchen. "What can I get you?"

"A Coke is fine, thanks," Anna called back. She considered whether she should sit on the couch or on the chair kitty-corner to it. But the chair wasn't really facing the TV. Besides, she was afraid he'd tease her about it, as if she was afraid to even sit on the couch with him.

Noah came back with two bottles of Coke and handed one to Anna. He sat a comfortable distance from Anna, picked up the remote, and clicked on the TV. The usual FBI warnings filled the giant screen, followed by a night skyline of Manhattan. "Alex and I wrote the first draft while we were still at Yale," Noah explained as the credits rolled.

Anna sipped her Coke. This was sort of fantastic, actually. She'd never before sat with an award-winning screenwriter, watching his movie. And Noah seemed like a nice guy. Not particularly "Hollywood," which Anna liked.

On-screen, the camera panned from the skyline to the streets and night morphed to day, the streets filling up with people in overdrive. "Wouldn't you be more comfortable if you put your feet up?" Noah suggested.

"No thanks, I'm fine," Anna said.

The camera followed a multiply-pierced girl with green hair into the Astor Place barbershop. She walked into the back and put her ratty backpack into a locker.

"That's Piper," Noah explained. "Hey, listen, I give the world's best foot massages. Put 'em up here."

Anna considered. Nothing wrong with a foot massage. She swiveled a little and lifted her legs into Noah's lap. It seemed innocent enough. He reached into a small drawer in the side table and brought out some jojoba oil. On-screen, Piper was explaining to the salon owner why she was late. In the bungalow, Noah Monahan was massaging Anna's right foot.

"God, your feet are perfect," Noah said.

Anna had never thought about it before. She had high arches—good for dancing. And they got her from point A to point B. "Thanks."

"Your toes are so elegant," Noah went on.

Elegant toes? Was this weird? Anna couldn't quite decide. Maybe she was overreacting. It wasn't like Noah had made a move on her. He was just massaging her foot. And doing a damned good job of it, too.

On the screen, Piper was getting a basin of soapy water to give a customer a pedicure. "Would you like that?" Noah asked Anna.

"Like what?"

"I could paint your toenails for you," he offered, his voice getting breathy.

Okay, that was *definitely* getting weird.

"That's nice of you, but no thanks." She tried to lower her legs, but Noah caught her right ankle and held it tight.

"Your feet are such a turn-on. Has anyone ever licked your toes?"

That was enough. Anna swung her legs back down and pushed into her sandals. "I have to go."

"Hey, listen, we don't have to—"

"Sorry, but I just remembered someplace I need to be." Anna got up and reached for her purse.

She babbled something or other by way of thanks, and she was out of there. Her heart was pounding as she headed back to the pool. Wait till she told Cyn. Back at the pool, Anna found Susan and Cammie deep in conversation. Fortunately, Alex was gone. Dee was in the pool, swimming laps. Anna joined her.

"Oh, hi, that was fast," Dee commented. "Didn't you like Noah?"

"He's fine," Anna said, not about to go into the details with Dee.

"I know, but he's no Ben, right?" Dee put her feet on the bottom of the pool and put her hands over her stomach.

Anna was not up for this. "You're not pregnant, Dee."

Dee's gaze wavered. "Well, I'm really, really late. And I'm never late. So if I *am*, it's Ben's. So did you talk to him?"

"Since when?"

"Since New Year's."

"No." What was the point of telling Dee the truth?

"I saw you with him at school today. It's really bad karma to lie, Anna."

Anna was regretting her decision to get in the water. This girl was maddening. "The point is, Ben and I are not together. We went out on one date. That's all."

Dee frowned. "I don't know whether to believe you."

"This is just a guess on my part, Dee, but maybe that's because no one you hang around with ever tells the truth. In fact, maybe it's contagious."

"Maybe," Dee agreed. "So you don't care that he and I hooked up?"

"No, Dee. I don't."

Whether that was completely true, Anna wasn't sure. But she started a powerful crawl toward the other end of the pool, doing a perfect kick turn at the far wall. That felt good. What didn't feel good was what she saw when her head broke the water again. It was Susan, laughing heartily at something that Cammie had just said.

"Did you bare your soles to each other, Anna?"

Cammie called out. "Did you play this-little-piggie-went-to-market?"

Anna reddened. So, Cammie knew about Noah's little fixation but hadn't bothered to warn her. Clearly she'd told Susan, though, who was joining in the giggling at her misadventure.

So much for wild and spontaneous.

Anna came home two hours later to find her father with his girlfriend, Margaret, on the tufted-silk living-room couch, eating Chinese takeout off Wedgwood china plates that had once belonged to Anna's great-grandmother.

"Would you like a plate, Anna?" her father asked. "There's plenty."

"Nice to see you again, Anna," Margaret added. Once again Anna was struck by the more than passing resemblance that Margaret Cunningham bore to Jane Percy: the same wheat-blond hair, the same tall and slender carriage, the same aristocratic features. Margaret was even wearing a Jane Percy–type outfit: fitted gray trousers and a black three-ply cashmere turtleneck.

"I had Django drive over to the Sam Woo in Van Nuys and bring it back," Jonathan explained. "Their curry shrimp is out of this world."

"Thanks, but I had a tuna sandwich with Susan." Anna sat in the antique wing chair opposite the couch.

"Your sister is *here*? In Los Angeles? She can't be here." Anna's intention to shock him had worked.

"Well, I just put her in a bungalow at the Beverly Hills Hotel, so I'd have to say it's possible."

"What about Hazelden?"

"She checked herself out."

"Christ. Of all the stupid, irresponsible—"

"Jonathan, calm down," Margaret chastised.

He swiped a weary hand over his face. "Is she at least sober?"

Anna nodded. "I think she's really trying, Dad."

"If she was really trying, her ass would still be in rehab!" He threw his balled-up napkin on the table in disgust. "Ask her to come see me, Anna. She and I need to talk."

"Pick up the phone and ask her yourself."

"You know she'll hang up on me," her father said. "The only one who has any influence with her is you."

Anna folded her arms. "She's very angry at you, you know."

"Well, I can't very well do anything about that if she won't see me, can I?"

There was silence for a few moments as Anna thought this over and realized that her father made a good point. "Okay," she conceded. "I'll talk to her tomorrow. I don't know if it'll make any difference, though. Excuse me." She headed for the stairs.

"Anna, a moment?" Margaret asked.

Anna turned back and waited.

"Your father told me how disappointed you were when the internship over at Randall Prescott's agency fell through," Margaret said. "I feel partly responsible for that—I had a terrible argument with him over one of his clients who jumped ship. He's filed suit, in fact."

"That's all right," Anna said automatically.

"Actually, it isn't, but it's kind of you to say so. In any event, I think your father has told you that I'm involved in a new startup called Apex. I'm partnering with a few maverick agents from CAA and Paradigm. We're all taking our clients with us—it will cause quite a stir in the trades tomorrow."

"I wish you the best of luck."

Margaret smiled. "Thank you, it's very exciting. Now, here's my point. There's going to be a lot of work to do. If you're still interested in an internship, we'd love to offer you the position. It'll be after school, though, not instead of it."

"Told you I'd come through," her father put in.

Anna was pleased despite the fact that if she accepted, she'd still have to attend high school classes. "That sounds great. What would I be doing?"

"Some of it will be sheer drudgery, I'm afraid. You're going to get to know the photocopy machine very well. But part of our mission is to turn young playwrights into screenwriters. Those young people need to get around town, be seen at the right places, and meet the right people. Believe me, they'd prefer to be seen with someone closer to their own age than their agent."

"That sounds . . . intriguing," Anna admitted.

"And of course, you'd have the opportunity to do a

lot of reading—we'd encourage that. Wouldn't want you escorting a writer around town without being familiar with his work. He'd loathe that."

"Or she," Anna added with a smile.

"Touché." Margaret tipped her head at Anna. "You and I will get along just fine."

"That's incredibly nice of you," Anna said.

Margaret laughed. "Why do you sound so surprised?"

Because I've disliked you from the first moment I saw you on New Year's Eve, for no better reason than that you're my father's girlfriend, Anna thought.

She didn't say it, though.

"I'm just pleased," were the perfect words she chose to utter.

"Good. Can you stop by after school tomorrow and meet everyone? Your dad has the address."

Ana turned toward the stairs again. "That's fine."

"You won't forget about talking to Susan, will you?" her father asked.

"No. In fact, I'll call her now."

Anna excused herself and went up to her room. She clicked on the TV as she got ready for bed. As she brushed her teeth in the bathroom, she heard, "And now we return to *Piper's Dream.*"

How ironic. Anna clicked off the TV. Sometimes fame and fortune just weren't what they were cracked up to be.

She was about to wash her face when she remembered about calling her sister. Just as she reached for the phone by her bed, it rang.

She picked it up. "Yes?"

"Don't hang up. Please."

Ben. Anna would know that voice anywhere. Her heart tap danced at double time. "Why are you calling me? There's nothing else to say."

"If you looked into my eyes, you'd know that isn't true."

"That's perfectly all right, I can use my imagination," she said frostily.

"Or you could look out your window."

She paused for a moment to absorb it all. It felt strange to be the object of such a dogged pursuit. When she felt ready, she went to the picture window that overlooked the back garden. There was gorgeous Ben in a pool of light, his electric blue eyes glowing in the evening sky. The balcony scene from *Romeo and Juliet* came to mind. *"Come, night; come, Romeo."* Anna had fallen in love with that play at age ten, when she'd seen it performed in a Broadway revival. She'd whispered Juliet's lines into her Belgian-lace-edged linen pillowcase and dreamed that one day she would love a boy and he would love her back as passionately as Juliet loved her Romeo.

Romeo and Juliet both ended up dead, Anna reminded herself now. *That's where fevered love gets you. Better to be with a guy like Adam, where there's not so much fire—*

"Will you come down? Please?" he asked.

"How did you get in without setting off the alarm?"

"Right after dinner the gate was open. I've been waiting for the light to go on in your room. Come down. Please?"

She hesitated. "What's the point?"

"Anna." His voice cracked with stress. "I can't eat, I can't sleep. I can't go back to school until I speak to you. Come on. We can't just end it like this. Didn't that night mean anything to you?"

Pain and anger flared inside her. He sounded like he was reciting lines from a bad soap opera. And damn him, it brought tears to her eyes anyway. "That's the whole point. It did."

"Then—"

"Shut up. And don't move." Anna clicked off the phone and pulled on a pair of jeans. She grabbed a sweatshirt, pushed into sandals, and headed for the door. At the last moment she stopped, went to her dresser, and sprayed herself with Chanel No. 5. If she was going to kiss him off forever, then dammit, she was going to kiss him off smelling great.

Anna went outside through the kitchen door. There was Ben, standing on the brick path that led to the gazebo, in jeans and a cable-knit sweater. The closer she got to him, the more her heart fluttered. She could actually hear the vibrations. "Anna."

Though she preferred to believe that it was the night chill in the air, the way he said her name made her shiver.

Mind over body, she told herself.

She took a deep breath before she addressed him. "Ben, I'm only here so you can look into *my* eyes when I tell you this for the last time. It's over."

"Why? I know you feel something for me—"

"Only because hormones have no conscience."

Ben looked stung. "It's more than that. You know it is."

"No, I don't. We don't really know each other. I had too much to drink on the plane. When we went out on New Year's Eve, I fell for the boy I wanted you to be. But you're not him."

"I *can* be that guy, Anna."

"Really?" She folded her arms. "Let's start with some honesty, then. Who is this mystery celebrity whose life you had to save on New Year's Eve?"

Ben rubbed his bloodshot eyes. "I can't say."

"Fine."

She turned to head back to the house, but Ben caught her wrist. "Come on, Anna. What kind of a schmuck would I be to tell you?"

"The kind who claims I mean something to him," Anna said, eyes flashing. "What do you think I'm going to do, post it on the Internet?"

"You can't be serious. You won't reconsider unless I tell you her name?"

"It's more than that. You have an excuse for everything. Why you had a relationship last year with a bitch like Cammie, why you ended up in bed with Dee, why you stranded me on New Year's Eve. And I'm sure there are a million more."

A muscle ticked in his jaw. "I'm sorry that I'm not perfect enough for you."

That statement hit Anna hard; it was so much like what Susan had said to her. *Was* she being unfair?

No, she decided. Ben was bound to break her heart over and over and over. Why should she say yes to that? Wasn't anyone in Los Angeles just . . . regular? Did *everyone* have some hidden agenda? Not everyone. Not Adam. He was so clearly the superior boy, the boy she *should* be with.

"Ben, you don't have to be anything, or do anything, for me," she said quietly. But her heart was still pounding as powerfully as it had the moment she'd heard his voice on the phone. "Not balloons, not roses, not phone calls. Nothing."

His eyes looked tortured. "Anna—"

"Stop. I can't do this." *It just hurts too much,* she added in her mind. "I'm asking you to leave me alone, Ben. I mean it." She turned around and went back as deliberately as she could to the house so Ben wouldn't have a chance to argue.

But back up in her room, she couldn't help herself. She went to the window and looked down at the backyard. And sure enough, he was still there, sitting on one of the stone benches along the walkway, his face buried in his hands. There was no denying it; in some ways, she felt exactly the same way he did.

Canine Love

Honk honk!

Adam downed the last of his orange juice and stuck his glass in the sink. The kitchen was all gleaming wood, with a giant oak table built by his dad's old college buddy. His mother, Linda, sat across from him at the table, drinking coffee and reading the *Los Angeles Times.* She was wearing a rust-colored velour sweatshirt that matched her perfectly coifed short red hair. She looked up at her son. "Scored a ride, I see," she said, smiling.

"Sam Sharpe." He picked up his backpack and looped it over one arm. Bowser jumped at him, tongue hanging out, panting hopefully. "No, Bowz, you can't come to school with me. Sorry."

"Right," Linda agreed as the mutt slunk away. "Everyone knows no dogs are allowed at Beverly Hills High."

Adam pointed at her playfully. "You made a sexist joke, Mom. Get NOW on the phone."

"I know my secret is safe with you. I thought maybe you'd get a lift with that girl you took to the beach the other night."

"Asking seemed too pitiful. I really need a car, Mom."

"Then I'd say you really need to get a job."

"Why can't you spoil me rotten like all the other mothers in Beverly Hills?"

"Because she has values and a conscience," his dad, Leonard, said as he bounded downstairs, dressed in a tasteful blue suit.

Honk honk!

"Gotta run, I'll whine about this later." Adam kissed his mom on the top of her head before he dashed out the door. While it was true that he desperately wanted a car, it was also true that he genuinely liked his parents. He'd seen the horror-show families of most of his Beverly Hills friends. Compared to them, his was like some fifties sitcom throwback: parents married for twenty years and still in love with each other. Parents who listened. Parents who cared.

"Morning," Adam said as he slid into Sam's red Jensen.

"Could we hold it down to one honk in the future?" Sam asked as she gunned the sports car out of his driveway.

"How about you just give me one of the family vehicles? You know, cut out the middleman," Adam joked.

Sam pulled onto Coldwater Canyon. "Come over and pick one out. My father has so many cars, he can't keep them straight. He'd probably claim it was stolen and collect the insurance."

"Uh, I think that's a felony, Sam. Thanks anyway."

It was a gorgeous morning: the sun was shining, the sky was clear, the smog was at a low ebb, and the temperature was in the low sixties. Adam felt so good that he started to sing along with Bono on Sam's CD player.

"Now I know why you didn't go out for choir," Sam said.

"What's pitch when you've got enthusiasm?"

Sam flicked her eyes at him before she turned onto Sunset Boulevard. "What are you so disgustingly happy about?"

"New friend, maybe."

"Does that translate to 'girl'?"

Adam laughed. He liked Sam, always had, since the first day he'd met her. When she wasn't pulling the diva thing because her father was you-know-who and wasn't feeling sorry for herself because her father was you-know-who, she really was a funny, smart girl.

"Anna Percy," Adam filled in.

"Oh, *really.*"

"Didn't you see us together in her car Monday?"

Sam nodded. "Yeah. But she didn't mention being madly in love with you yet."

"She confides in you?" Adam asked.

"Not really," Sam said blithely, not mentioning that Anna had told her about sharing a kiss with Adam. One thing about growing up in Hollywood—information was a precious commodity.

Adam hadn't been in Los Angeles as long as Sam, but

he also had learned when to share and when not to. He wasn't going to tell Sam the truth—that he couldn't stop thinking about Anna. Not that he was big on playing it cool—the only place he liked to play games was on the b-ball court. It was more about being shy. He'd had girl-friends before. There was Julie Hewser, back in Michigan. She was sweet, smart, really a great girl. But when she'd told him that she loved him, it had made him uncomfort-able because he didn't feel like he could say those words back. After a while she'd wanted them to have sex so she could, as she put it, "prove her love." He hadn't done that, either, despite the real temptation of Julie in lace underwear at his parents' lake house. So he drove her home, she called him the biggest loser in the world, and that had been the end of that. He'd never told any of his buddies the story for fear they would corroborate Julie's accusation.

When he'd moved to Beverly Hills, he'd been under the radar until the girls had seen what a stud he was on the basketball court. Then they'd flocked to him. He'd dated one of the cheerleaders, a really cute girl named Tabitha whose idea of fun was sneaking into the White Lotus club with a fake ID and seeing how many celebri-ties she could get to talk to her. When she'd told him she thought *Jonathan Livingston Seagull* was the greatest novel ever written, he'd known it was time to move on. Then there was Sam Sharpe. They'd made out a little on New Year's Eve, and Adam thought she was one of the brightest girls he'd ever met. But she seemed to be pre-tending it had never happened, so he went with the flow.

And now there was Anna. Which, frankly, made it easy not to think about Sam.

Yes, Anna had kissed him, but she hadn't called him the night before. And when he'd called her at her father's house, there'd been no answer. What if she didn't even like him back all that much?

"We took the dog to the beach."

"Yeah, but I bet your dream life about her is a lot juicier," Sam guessed.

Adam could feel himself blushing. Because as usual, Sam was on the nose. "Hey, out of my dreams and into my car," Adam quipped, quoting an old Billy Ocean song. For some strange reason, on certain days his inner radio was tuned to lite FM. "That is, if I *had* a car."

"Well, the grand theft auto concept is still open," Sam said. "Oh, look, there's your object of lust now." Sam cocked her head toward the front steps of the school. "Let's go tell her you want to jump her bones. Kidding. Catch you later."

"Thanks for the ride!" Adam called after her as Sam veered off to the side entrance where she usually met up with Dee and Cammie before classes started. He sprinted to catch up with Anna. "Morning!"

She looked happy to see him. A good sign, as signs go. "Hi, Adam."

They walked into school together. Adam took in the beauty that was Anna Percy and realized she was more dressed up than usual, in elegant black pants and what looked to Adam to be a white cashmere turtleneck. "Wow, you look great," he said.

"Thanks." They dodged through the crowded hallway, heading toward Anna's locker. "I have a meeting after school about an internship at an agency. I was trying to dress the part."

"Sounds great, I hope it works out." They stopped in front of her locker, and she spun her combination. "So, listen," he went on, hoping to strike the right casual tone. "How about joining me and Bowser for a run up in Runyon Canyon—it's like Hollywood's unofficial dog park. He said that if I didn't invite you, he was going on a hunger strike."

"How about if you come and hang out while I go to this meeting?" Anna suggested, storing some books in her locker and extracting others. "It shouldn't take very long—it's just a meet and greet, I think. Then I'll change, we'll pick up the canine love of my life, and go. Is it far?"

"Up that way." Adam pointed toward the hills above Laurel Canyon. "Sounds cool. And as an added bonus, I won't have to grovel for a ride home."

Anna laughed. "I knew you had ulterior motives."

Adam's mind was going a million miles an hour. *She must like me, or she wouldn't have said yes so quickly. But what kind of like?*

"Well, well, look what we have here."

Adam turned; Cammie and Dee were approaching them. "Adam Flood and Anna Percy. Aren't they just too cute for words?" Cammie asked Dee rhetorically.

"Sam says you guys are a couple now," Dee told Anna and Adam. "That's so sweet!"

Adam was ready to kill Sam. He didn't even have the nerve to look at Anna. "We're *friends*," he corrected. "What's up?"

Cammie pushed her white Armani sunglasses up into her hair. "Not much. We're going to Bev's after school. Maybe you two would like to come."

"Who's Bev?" Anna asked.

Cammie laughed. "God, you really are FOB."

Anna shook her head, not comprehending.

"FOB means fresh off the boat," Adam translated. "And Bev's is what everyone calls the Beverly Hills Hotel."

"Ah." Anna smiled.

"We've got a favorite waiter there," Dee said. "He'll bring us drinks."

"In the middle of the afternoon?" he asked lightly. "Living dangerously."

"Well, I'm not drinking right now, for personal reasons." Dee gave Anna a significant look—Adam had no idea what that was about. "But you guys can."

"Oh, Adam, I adore you. You're so flyover," Cammie cooed.

"Flyover, the part of the country you fly over when you go from New York to Los Angeles," Adam translated for Anna. "Where people watch *Seventh Heaven* and aren't embarrassed to admit it."

Cammie sidled up to him and kissed him on the

cheek. "I think it's charming. And I envy the girl who's the first one to do the deed with you. I bet inside that point guard is an Energizer Bunny."

Adam laughed, though he realized at the same time that Cammie had correctly assessed him as a virgin— one of the last ones in Beverly Hills, evidently. "I doubt that's something you'll ever find out, Cammie."

"Ooh, he shoots and scores," Cammie announced, sports commentator–style.

"Anyway, we already have plans after school," Anna added.

"All righty, then," Cammie singsonged. "We'll give our regards to your sister."

"My sister? What do you want with her?" Anna asked sharply.

"Anna, relax. We're going to the hotel, she's staying at the hotel, and we'll probably see her at the pool. What's the problem?" Cammie asked reasonably.

Anna's voice was stony. "I don't have a problem. She's just very fragile right now. I'd hope even you could understand that."

"She seemed fine last night," Cammie said with a shrug. "Whatever. So, have a blast later, you two, wherever you're going."

Anna stared at Cammie and Dee, shaking her head as they departed.

"Your sister's in town?" Adam asked as they headed for his locker.

Anna's face seemed to darken. "It's complicated."

Adam wasn't sure if this was Anna's way of inviting him to probe further or her polite way of telling him to mind his own business.

But before he could find out more, the first-period bell rang.

The Perfect Intern

"The test of a first-rate intelligence is the ability to hold two opposed ideas in the mind at the same time, and still retain the ability to function."

Anna reread the line from F. Scott Fitzgerald's famous series of essays called *The Crack-Up* for perhaps the tenth time. Mrs. Breckner had allowed her to spend English class in the library so she could work on her Gatsby project.

The words were captivating—Anna knew that they could be the jumping-off place for her short film . . . but she still didn't know exactly how they'd translate to the screen. Fitzgerald, Anna figured, had been referring to the dualities in his own life that he'd applied to Jay Gatsby— the loving and hating of money, the attraction to the life of the very rich and the repulsion at its hypocrisy. It made Anna wonder about herself and her own dualities, but not in a way that had anything to do with money or lifestyle. It was more like the opposing ideas of Ben and Adam and how they fit into her life. Which had nothing to do with the script she was supposed to be writing. Unless—

What if . . . her script was about a wealthy girl struggling with her identity? On the one hand, she longed for a passionate, dangerous adventure—Ben. But on the other, she sought the comfort of a safer relationship—Adam. The girl would be caught between two boys. She could work in the Palm Springs spa background footage as a way of fleshing out the world of her protagonist and show the dualities of the cult of wealthy self-absorption at the same time.

I like it.

Anna began to type away on her laptop. Sam had given her a bunch of screenplays by famous Hollywood writers—*Piper's Dream,* among them—and some special software, so she knew what she wrote would at least look professional. The character names Alana, Berkeley, and Aaron flew into her head—she had no idea why. Soon she was lost in her own story—Alana at a Hollywood party like the ones Anna had attended on New Year's Eve, courted first by Berkeley, then by Aaron, unable to make up her mind about who to leave with.

It wasn't until the final bell rang that Anna looked up from her laptop. She backed up what she'd written and went to meet Adam in the student parking lot, as they'd agreed. If it hadn't been for her appointment at Apex, she would have been happy to stay in the library and continue writing.

Adam looked so cute, leaning against her Lexus, waiting for her. She was so giddy over her idea for the script that she impetuously gave him a light kiss on the lips.

"Nice to see you, too," he said, grinning.

As Anna pulled out of the parking lot, going toward Wilshire Boulevard, she bubbled over with ideas about her screenplay. It just felt so good to be excited again about something that didn't involve guys—except on the page, of course.

"I realize it's only a short," Anna said as she headed toward Westwood Boulevard. "But it's exciting to think that I'll actually get to see it filmed. Sam said we can use her father's editing room."

"Cool. I guess this means we're not going to San Diego this weekend, though."

"You should come out to the desert," Anna said. "That is, if you want to. You can meet my sister—she's coming, too."

"You were going to tell me about her," Adam reminded her.

Anna nodded, then hesitated.

"Highly evolved guy that I am, I sense that something's wrong," Adam said. "Is it about your sister?"

Anna knew it was ridiculous, but she couldn't bring herself to open up. "I'll tell you about it some other time," she said lightly. Then she opened the center console between her seat and Adam's—it was full of CDs. When Django had seen that her father had leased her the Lexus, he'd brought over an eclectic assortment of music—Anna hadn't even heard of most of the artists. She pointed to the CDs. "Pick something. Loud."

Adam held up a CD. "Coldplay. Check it out." He popped the music into the player; a gut-wrenching ballad filled her head and her car. She told him to crank it up to drown out her tumbling thoughts.

Minutes later they pulled into the underground lot at the corner of Westwood and Le Conte, directly below the building that housed the Apex office. One of the city's ubiquitous valets took her car, and she and Adam rode the elevator to the main lobby, which was enormous. The windows went from floor to ceiling, and tall plants encircled the entire space. From the middle of the ceiling hung a huge Lichtenstein painting, and all the furniture was chrome. She felt like she was on the set of some futuristic movie from the 1960s. Anna signed in with security and was given a visitor's tag, which she promptly shoved into her pocket.

"Look, I know this neighborhood. I'll go get coffee at Jerry's Deli. It's right around the corner. Come meet me when you're done," Adam offered.

"I'm sure there's a reception area where you can wait."

"Nah. You should go up alone. Good luck."

"Thanks." Anna took the elevator to the twelfth floor, where it opened into a spacious foyer that still smelled of wet paint. A stunningly beautiful young woman with cropped black hair and green eyes sat with headphones on behind a massive circular desk. "Good afternoon, Apex, hold, please. Good afternoon, Apex . . . I'll transfer you. Good afternoon, Apex, hold, please."

Then, letting the phones ring for a few moments, the girl looked up at Anna. "Yes?"

"I'm Anna Percy. I have an appointment at three o'clock to see Margaret Cunningham."

The girl pushed a button on her console and spoke into her headset briefly before turning back to Anna. "She'll be right with you. May I get you anything? Coffee? A Coke? Bottled water?"

"No thanks." Anna took a seat on a low-slung gray leather couch and glanced at the trade papers on an end table: *Variety*, *Hollywood Reporter*, and *Publishers Weekly*. A travel magazine caught Anna's eye. On the cover was a Mediterranean-style inn on a windswept beach. Just looking at it made Anna feel more relaxed. She flipped open to the article. The Montecito Inn. In Santa Barbara, about an hour and a half north of Los Angeles. Built by Charlie Chaplin to accommodate his visiting friends. It looked so peaceful, so serene. Anna could picture herself walking the beach, her jeans rolled up, listening to the ocean. For a big-city girl, she was inordinately fond of non-big-city places.

"Anna Percy?" A diminutive Asian woman in an Armani suit had come out for her.

"Yes." Anna stood up.

"I'm Wei Ling Feinberg, Margaret's assistant." She shook Anna's hand. "Did you have any trouble finding us?"

"No, not at all."

"Good. Want some coffee? A Coke? Bottled water?"

Anna declined. "Well, come with me," Wei Ling

instructed. "It's still a sea of boxes, so watch your step."

Anna followed the assistant through a set of double doors and down a long hallway, passing a glassed-in conference room with a view of the Santa Monica Mountains. As they walked, she could hear snippets of phone conversations—most of them extremely profane—from inside various offices.

"Those schmucks screwed Al and Miles on *Hysteria*, so now they can bite me. I've got a long memory, Bob—"

"Tell your asshole of a boss that he'd better take my goddamn call, or you'll never temp in this town again."

"So what if her play is in previews? They're offering two hundred and fifty for her to polish the script, and she doesn't even have to do a good job."

Margaret's office was at the end of the hall. It faced west, toward Brentwood, Santa Monica, and the ocean beyond. Though workmen were laying a Navajo-pattern carpet, Margaret sat placidly behind her steel-and-marble desk. When she saw Anna, she rose gracefully and came to the door. "Anna, I see you found the madhouse. Did Wei Ling offer you anything?"

"Yes, thanks." Anna turned to the assistant, but she'd already disappeared.

"Coming through." Two workmen were hauling an enormous framed poster for *One Flew Over the Cuckoo's Nest* toward the doorway; Margaret and Anna had to step aside to let them pass.

Margaret sighed. "Why don't we go to the conference room? I think it's the only quiet spot right now."

They headed back the way Anna had come—Margaret stopping at a few offices to introduce Anna to various employees. Finally they landed in the conference room. It could seat twenty comfortably at a long table surrounded by buttery leather high-backed chairs. Anna drifted over to the floor-to-ceiling wall of windows: the room featured the same view as Margaret's office. But looking down, she could see just the edge of the Los Angeles National Cemetery, with its countless rows of soldiers' headstones gleaming white against the green grass.

Margaret shut the door, and the jangly energy of the Apex office turned to relative tranquility. "Please." Margaret sat in a big chair at the head of the table and gestured Anna into a place to her right. "So, Anna. Would it be safe to assume that you know how to use e-mail and a copying machine?"

Anna smiled. "Yes."

Margaret touched her arm. "We'll try not to load you down with too much scut work. Frankly, with your looks and pedigree, we can make better use of you out there." She gestured toward the window. "And I guarantee it will be much more fun. Are you game?"

"Absolutely," Anna said enthusiastically.

"How about reading screenplays and books? Interested in writing coverage?"

"Sorry, I don't know what that is."

Margaret laughed. "Let me fill you in on a Hollywood not-so-big secret. In this town, none of the big execs read. They get their youngest staffers to read books and screenplays—and write up summaries for them. That's called coverage."

"But how can they tell whether or not it's any good?" Anna wondered. "I mean, it's all in the writing, isn't it?"

"Unfortunately, a lot of producers don't consider writers very high on the food chain," Margaret said. "Which is one of the reasons so many high-concept god-awful films get made. Here at Apex, though, we have great respect for the written word."

Anna nodded. It did sound interesting. And maybe it would help her with her own writing.

"Wonderful. Well, we've got a closet full of scripts and bound galleys and fifty file drawers full of coverage summaries you can learn from. Help yourself. If you take something, just put it back. Anyway, I'm a jump-right-in kind of woman and we're a jump-right-in kind of agency. One of my clients—a playwright from New York—just got hired off a pitch to write a script for Touchstone."

"Pitch?" Anna asked.

"Sorry, another term of art. He had an idea that we thought was salable, so I set up some meetings for him at the big studios. Paramount passed, but that was no shocker. Warners passed, and that surprised me. But Touchstone Pictures bit. Anyway, I got him a fabulous deal, mid–six figures against low seven. He went back to Manhattan to buy an apartment, and he's coming back out here on Saturday. The Steinbergs are giving a big Maxomile party in the hills on Sunday. We'd like you to escort him there."

The name Steinberg meant nothing to Anna, but she figured she could research it. Still, she was surprised at Margaret's suggestion. "I'd be happy to. But shouldn't it be someone with more experience?"

Margaret waved a dismissive hand. "He's a twenty-one-year-old boy wonder with the maturity of an eggplant, but he's also bloody brilliant. Believe me, Brock will be thrilled to see you."

Anna was taken aback. Brock was such an uncommon name. Could it possibly be . . . ?

"Margaret, are you talking about Brock Franklin?"

"Yes, exactly."

Anna laughed. "I know him."

It was Margaret's turn to look surprised. "How is that?"

"He went to Trinity, where my sister, Susan, and I went. He was a senior when Susan was a junior. I think maybe they went out once or twice."

"Well, this is fantastic, isn't it?" Margaret marveled. "Clearly I've chosen the perfect intern. I don't have details yet on time and place, but as soon as I know—"

The conference room door slammed open and a tall, middle-aged man with blondish hair and a deep tan barged in. "Dammit, Margaret, we need you on this call," he fairly spat. "Artisan is trying to fuck us on the fucking deal. Again."

"Fine, I'll be right in. Clark, this is our new intern, Anna Percy. Anna, this is Clark. She—"

"Fucking Artisan," the man interrupted her. "One fucking hit and they think they're Jack Warner. It's now or never, Margaret." He turned around, slamming the door on his way out.

"Manners aren't his long suit," Margaret said wryly. "But he's got a client list a mile long." She stood. "Sorry to cut this short."

Anna rose, too. "Thanks for your time. I'm looking forward to working here."

"Lovely." She held the door open for Anna. "Be sure to ask Tamara at the desk to validate you. I'll be in touch."

Margaret shook Anna's hand. Anna didn't understand that last part about Tamara and validating, so she just found her way back to the elevators to the ground floor. When the doors opened, she was surprised to see Adam standing by the guard's desk, reading the sports section of the *Los Angeles Times.*

"Hi," he said. "Jerry's was closed—some movie of the week is shooting there. So I came back. I didn't want you to get lost."

Anna smiled. "That was considerate."

"Didn't take long," he said, folding the newspaper and putting it under his arm.

"No, but it looks like it's going to be great." They walked to the elevator that serviced the parking garage. "I get to take Brock Franklin to a party on Sunday."

"Should I know who he is?"

"No, not really. He wrote a hit play about crass and callow Upper East Side rich kids and got a million-dollar deal from it, evidently." Anna chuckled. "Not that he needs another million dollars."

"How would you know?"

"My sister and I went to school with him. You've heard of the Franklin Mint? Same family."

"Well, that's convenient. What else?"

The elevator came and they stepped into it.

"I met one of Margaret's partners," Anna went on. "Well, *met* is the wrong word. We were in the same room briefly, though he never looked at me. And his favorite word was *fuck*. Clark something or other, I think his name was. Then someone named Tamara was supposed to validate me, whatever that means."

The elevator door opened onto the parking level. "Whoa, back up one," Adam suggested. "Clark Sheppard?"

"I don't know. Maybe." Anna found her parking ticket and gave it to the valet. He told her it was ten dollars, and she paid for her parking. "I think so."

"Blond hair, deep tan, on the tall side?"

"Yes," Anna said. "Why?"

"Sheppard," Adam repeated. "Doesn't that last name ring a bell?"

She had to think for a moment. And then, suddenly, she knew.

"Oh, shit."

"Oh yeah. He's Cammie's father."

The attendant brought Anna's car around and they got in. "Well, hopefully I'll never have to work for him specifically," Anna said.

"From what I hear, *everyone* works for him. He's that kind of guy."

"I guess I'll find out," Anna said. "What's that part about getting validated by Tamara?"

"It's the part about saving yourself ten bucks. Tamara is probably the receptionist. Validate means to stamp your parking ticket so that you park for free."

"Phew. I was concerned it meant validate my self-worth," Anna added wryly.

Adam cranked Coldplay back up as Anna headed back to Wilshire Boulevard. So Cammie's father was one of the partners in the agency where she'd be interning. It got her thinking about his daughter and her alleged interest in a friendship with Susan.

"Adam, do you mind if we make a stop at the Beverly Hills Hotel? On our way back?"

"I don't suppose you're inviting me to take a room and ravish you."

"A bit premature."

"Hey, a guy can dream."

"My sister is staying there. I just want to stop in and say hi."

"Yeah, sure," Adam said easily, but there was a question in his eyes.

"It's . . ." Anna stopped. But she knew she was being ridiculous. Susan's problems were hardly state secrets. So *what* if it was personal family information?

I am not my mother, Anna reminded herself.

"My sister, Susan, has had some problems lately. With alcohol."

"Welcome her to Los Angeles—she'll fit right in."

"But Cammie and Dee are such party girls . . ."

Adam nodded. "I see your point."

"So it's okay with you if—?"

"Sure," Adam said. "Hey, maybe your sister will want to come meet Bowser. But I have to warn you, he's a one-woman dog. And his heart already belongs to you."

But when they got to the hotel, Susan wasn't in her room, and the valet reported that her car wasn't in the lot. Anna tried to convince herself that she didn't mind. She'd spend a little time with Adam, take the dog for a walk up in the canyon, and then go home and work on her screenplay. Maybe she'd even e-mail it over to Sam for notes. Susan could take care of herself.

Probably.

Retail Therapy

At that moment Susan was with Cammie Sheppard at the Beverly Center, a multiple-story upscale mall in West Hollywood. They were on an impromptu shopping expedition. True, the Beverly Center had its share of tacky chain-store outlets, but there were also some more-than-decent boutiques, and the mall attracted visitors from all over the world. Cammie and her friends considered it a spectator sport to watch tourists *ooh* and *aah* as they wandered from shop to shop.

Cammie believed in retail therapy. She knew it was a cliché, but what better way to forget about her own problems than to acquire something—or somethings—new to wear? That Anna was unhappy about Cammie befriending Susan made the shopping expedition that much more delicious. That Ben and Anna were no longer BenandAnna was only a small comfort. The humiliation she'd endured on New Year's Eve, when she'd done everything but give Ben a lap dance to try and get him back, wasn't likely to go away so easily. Simply put, Anna had screwed Cammie by screwing Ben. And Cammie couldn't forgive that.

"Oh, try this on, Susan. It'll look great on you!" They were in the Betsey Johnson boutique, where Cammie held up a stretchy, low-cut black net top with four inches of fringe that began just under the bust.

"Black is my color, but the fringe is kind of tacky," Susan mused. So far, she hadn't seen a thing that appealed to her.

"You're going for a kind of rich-girl biker-chick thing, right?" Cammie pawed through another rack of tops and held up a hot pink camisole. "You sure you don't do color?"

Susan shrugged, touching a purple minidress with the middle cut out. "It's all just too . . . *colorful.*"

"Then *this* is perfect," Cammie decreed, thrusting a slinky jet-black top at Susan. Susan took it and thoughtfully held it up against herself, then frowned. "I don't even have to try it on; it's too small." She groaned. "God, I'm a size eight."

"You sound like my friend Sam," Cammie said, oozing sincerity. "Don't you think it's important for us women to be more accepting of our bodies? You shouldn't dis yourself like that."

"Rehab carbs," Susan said, sighing. "I always look like a pig when I get out."

Cammie gave God a mental high five. How lucky could she get? Anna's sister had just finished with rehab? Life was looking better and better all the time. "Oh God, I know just what you mean," she agreed. "I gained like eight pounds *my* last time in."

"No shit, you were in rehab?"

Cammie tried to look contrite. "I don't like it to get around, but yeah."

"I just did Hazelden. Where were you?"

"Sierra Vista," Cammie said, automatically naming the Arizona rehabilitation facility where her father had ordered so many of his clients to go and dry out.

"Wow. I hear it's rugged there. What was your thing?"

"What wasn't? Sex, drugs, alcohol," Cammie confided. "I was an equal opportunity abuser."

"Tell me about it," Susan agreed. "I haven't been away from Hazelden for more than few days, but I'd kill for a shot of vodka. Not Stoli. Flagman. Iced. Liquid bliss."

"Totally," Cammie agreed. She spotted a pair of black pants and lifted them off the rack. "But it's not a good idea. Listen, we should change the subject. They told me in rehab that the worst possible thing to do is to start talking with another addict about how much you liked your drug of choice. Hey, why don't you try these pants? Then we can hit M·A·C. I'm out of Spice lip pencils."

Susan smiled and took the pants from Cammie. "Okay. Be right back."

"You got it," Cammie said.

No, she thought as Susan disappeared into one of the changing rooms. *I've* got *it. Actually, I've got her. Hook, line, and sinker. All I have to do is reel her in, anytime I want to.*

Cousin Alexis

"So, how many movie stars do you know?" Alexis asked Ben as they strolled down the Santa Monica promenade. It was a gorgeous evening, in the low seventies, and the outdoor parts of the restaurants were all full. They passed a mime playing a harmonica and two kids tap-dancing on a makeshift cardboard stage.

Ben had to laugh. His cousin Alexis, who lived in Salt Lake City, Utah, of all places, had just turned fifteen. With her glossy auburn hair falling over one eye and cargo pants that bared inches of taut midriff, she could easily have passed for twenty—that is, until she opened her mouth. Then she sounded more like she was twelve.

"Oh, dozens," Ben teased.

"Stop!" She playfully bumped her hip into him. "I'm serious!"

Alexis and her parents hadn't been to Los Angeles to visit Ben's family for three years, and she was so excited, she could barely keep from skipping down the promenade.

"Okay, I know a couple," Ben admitted. "But I'm not name-dropping."

"Aw, c'mon," Alexis wheedled as they strolled past a Banana Republic and a street vendor selling silver earrings. "Please?"

"Jackson Sharpe. In fact, I was just at his wedding."

"Wow!" Alexis breathed. "That is so cool. I mean he's really old and everything, but still. So what was the wedding like? Who was there?"

Anna was there, Ben thought. Why did every road seem to lead to her?

"Was Jennifer Aniston there?" Alexis prompted. "Or Beyonce? Oh my God, I would kill to meet her. Or how about Tobey Maguire? He is so hot."

"Nope," Ben said. "But . . . let's see. Mike Myers was there. And Jim Carrey. And Nicole Kidman."

"Get *out!*" Alexis exclaimed. "Oh my God, did you dance with Nicole?"

I danced with Anna, Ben thought. He could see her in his mind's eye: flaxen hair flowing to her shoulders, swinging against her high cheekbones. The elegance of her slender neck. The spot just between her collarbones where he'd kissed her—

"So did you?" Alexis interrupted.

"I had a date," Ben explained.

Suddenly, as if thinking about Anna had conjured her up, he saw her heading toward him. She was almost all the way down the block with some guy, laughing. No, it couldn't be her. It was just some other tall, lithe blonde—

She came closer. It really was her. And she was with Adam Flood. Their arms were linked. They looked so happy.

It was like a fist to Ben's gut. So that was the real reason she'd blown him off. She was with Adam. Damn. Why couldn't it be some asshole? Adam was a good guy, even though, at the moment, Ben wished he would curl up and die.

"That girl is looking at you," Alexis said, jutting her chin toward Anna. "Do you know her?"

"Do me a favor, Al, pretend you're my girlfriend, okay?" Ben asked.

"Yeah, I guess," she said with a shrug. "But why?"

"Tell you later. And I'll owe you one. Anna!" he called. Ben and Alexis headed for Anna and Adam. Ben quickly introduced everyone. He put his arm around Alexis's shoulders. She did her part by nuzzling against him.

"So, what are you guys up to?" Ben asked, as if running into Anna meant about as much to him as running into, say, Sam.

"We went up to Runyon Canyon with my dog," Adam explained. "Then I introduced Anna to Pink's World Famous."

"Standing in line to get hot dogs was a new experience," Anna added. She seemed nervous. Her eyes flicked over to Alexis, then back to Ben. "How about you two?"

"Oh, we just spent the afternoon making out," Alexis said blithely. "We were at Johnny Rockets, and this couple in the next booth yelled, 'Get a room!' So—"

"She's joking," Ben put in quickly.

"You two seem perfect for each other," Anna said, her voice going frosty.

"You guys, too," Ben forced himself to say.

Adam shoved his hands into the pockets of his jeans. "So, when are you going back to Princeton, Ben?"

"He can't," Alexis replied before Ben could. "He just keeps dragging me off to bed."

"Well, in that case you're definitely his type," Anna said. She threaded her arm through Adam's again. "We'd better go get the Streetheart tickets before they're sold out," she told Adam.

"They're doing a sunset show on the pier," Adam explained to Ben. "Killer blues band. You know 'em?"

"I've heard of them," Ben said vaguely. "So, have fun. Nice running into you guys," he added, hoping it sounded genuine.

"Same here," Adam said, putting an arm around Anna's shoulders.

Ben grabbed Alexis's waist. "Yeah. See you." Ben and Alexis continued down the promenade. Only when they reached the corner did he remove his hand from his cousin's waist.

"I get it. You wanted to make that girl jealous, right?" Alexis asked.

"Something like that."

"She's gorgeous."

Ben sighed. "I know."

"So was she your girlfriend or something?" Alexis prompted.

"I went out with her once."

"But now she's with that guy, Adam, huh? That sucks. I mean, it's totally obvious from the look on your face that you're madly in love with her."

"Yeah, well, seeing is believing," Ben stated. "She's with Adam now. The end."

"If you want her back, you should fight for her," Alexis decided. "That's what would happen in the movies."

"Except that this is real life."

"Nuh-uh," Alexis said. "This is Los Angeles. Nothing here is real. You're the one who told me that. So buy me a triple-dip ice cream cone and I'll tell you how to get your girlfriend back."

Ben swerved back toward the ice cream parlor they'd just passed. "Yes on the ice cream, no on the advice."

"But—"

"But nothing," Ben insisted, holding the door open for his cousin. They wove through the crowd and got in line. "You can't beat a dead horse, and this pony has gone to pony heaven."

"Speak English," Alexis demanded.

"I mean it's over." Ben had to force himself to say it. "When it comes to Anna Percy, I blew it. And I have no one to blame but myself."

The Same Boring Preppie Types

Anna trod the now-familiar path to Susan's bungalow at the Beverly Hills Hotel. The only sound was the *thwack-thwack-thwack* of rackets on balls as people played tennis on the lighted hotel courts. Why, why, why did she have to run into Ben and his new girlfriend? The images were seared into Anna's brain. Shimmering auburn hair, deep tan, convex stomach—she was Anna's physical opposite. She shouldn't care. She knew she shouldn't. So why did she feel so awful? What streak of masochism made her want a boy who was bad for her? She should be thinking about Adam. They'd had such a great day together.

Anna wanted to scream. To think that Ben had tried to get her back when he already had a new girlfriend! What a jerk! She clenched her eyes shut for a moment, as if to will away the Ben thoughts. She'd think about Susan. It was so much easier to worry about her sister's problems than to obsess about her own.

Susan was such an enigma these days. She was smart, probably even smarter than Anna was. Susan graduated fourth in her class. She'd been accepted by every college to which she'd applied, including Harvard. But she'd chosen Bowdoin College, in Maine, so that she could study with a certain famous historian who taught there.

At first she did great. Then things changed. She'd suddenly stopped going to class and started hanging out with the kids who majored in drugs and alcohol. She transferred to NYU, fell in love with a rock-and-roll guitarist from Ireland, and dropped out of school to follow the guy's band on a low-rent East Coast tour. And then the relationship ended. After that, Susan went back to Avenue D, in the East Village.

To this day, Anna had no idea what had happened at Bowdoin that had made Susan change. It made Anna sad. In a family where everyone was notoriously distant from everyone else, there had been a time when Anna and Susan had shared secrets and been each other's refuge. But that felt like a long, long time ago.

As Anna approached Susan's bungalow, she could hear the Wallflowers—one of the few rock bands she could identify—blaring through the windows, a sure sign that Susan had returned from wherever she'd been. She knocked discreetly on the door.

"Coming!" she heard Susan's muffled shout through the door. A moment later the door swung open—Susan was wearing the plush, monogrammed white terry robe the hotel provided every guest; her wet hair was wrapped in a towel. "Anna! I thought you were room service."

"No. Just me."

"Come in, I ordered enough for two. Have you eaten?"

"Hot dogs with a friend."

"My little sister, slumming it," Susan teased. "I'm impressed. Come on in."

Anna winced as she stepped into the bungalow. It looked so much like Noah Monahan's, she couldn't shake the image of him trying to seduce her feet. The bungalow featured a fully equipped kitchen, spacious living and dining rooms, and a bedroom with a four-poster bed. Through the open door to the bedroom Anna could see shopping bags of many sizes on the floor. "You went shopping?" she asked.

"With Cammie Sheppard," Susan said. "It was fun, in a mindless kind of way. I don't know why you don't like her, Anna. She's a hoot."

"Just be careful around her."

Susan shrugged, took the towel off her head, and went to the bathroom to blow-dry her hair. "You think too much and you worry too much," Susan decreed.

Was that true? Anna wondered. Probably. It was like she couldn't cut off the running monologue in her head. Sometimes she envied people who could just *be*.

There were three discreet knocks at the door.

"Now, that's gotta be room service," Susan said, reversing course. A check through the peephole confirmed her guess, and Susan opened the door for the waiter, who wheeled in a dining cart featuring a centerpiece of lavender and white orchids.

"Crab cake appetizer, lobster bisque, club sandwich

with extra bacon, fries, avocado-and-mango salad, hazel-nut cheesecake, and a Coke," he enumerated, lifting silver covers off various dishes and setting them down on the dining room table. "Can I get you anything else, miss?"

"No, that's fine, thanks." Susan scribbled her signature on the check, added a generous tip, and let the waiter out. She turned to Anna, red-faced. "Like I said, you caught me in a major pig-out. So now you have to help me eat."

"I'm not hungry," Anna protested.

"Come on. Save me from humiliation."

Anna laughed. "Okay, sure. I'll call it dessert."

They sat down together. The waiter had assumed the order was for two people, so extra plates had been provided. Anna took a plate and a section of the club sandwich and bit into it. "Delicious. So, what did you do besides go shopping?"

"Nothing." Susan cut into the crab cakes. "Cammie wanted to go club-hopping tonight, but I'm still kind of jet-lagged, so I bowed out."

"That was smart."

"I'm okay around alcohol, Anna."

"I never said you weren't."

"It's the tone. You sound just like Mom." She licked some mayonnaise from her pinkie.

"Do I?" Anna felt stricken.

"No, I'm sorry." Susan reached over to squeeze Anna's hand. "God, why do I do that? I get so defensive around you sometimes."

"Maybe that's how I make you feel," Anna said guiltily.

Susan shrugged and cut another bite of crab cake. "What can I tell you? You've got it. Mom's got it. And I don't. Guys love it. It's one of the reasons Dad fell in love with her."

Anna reached for Susan's Coke. "Speaking of. I was supposed to ask you to call him."

"I told you, Anna, I don't want to see him. Or speak to him."

"Okay, fine, you don't like him, I got that. But he's trying to change. Why can't you give him a chance?"

"Because."

"'Because'? What kind of answer is 'because'?"

"Did it ever occur to you, little sister, that I might know some things you don't know about Daddy dearest? And that for once I might be protecting you instead of the other way around?"

No, such a thing had never occurred to her. "What things?"

Susan waved her hand dismissively. "Forget it. Eat. Then come look at the cute clothes Cammie talked me into buying. We have to go wild this weekend so I can show 'em off. In fact, come see them now."

Susan led Anna into the bedroom and showed off her purchases—a sleeveless mauve Prada blouse with ruffles, an orange Marc Jacobs jacket with oversized buttons, a Diane von Furstenberg wraparound dress in a tiger print, and an Ann Demeulemeester skirt that

Anna couldn't quite figure out. It gathered at the waist and was cut at an extreme angle at the hem—where could anyone wear such a thing? Her sister's style was suddenly all over the map.

"I've turned into a fashion schizoid," Susan confessed. "But you have to admit, these black pants are hot." She slipped into them to show Anna. "What do you think?"

They were lacy and partially sheer. Anna could never wear a garment remotely like them. Well, not never. She'd worn much cheesier pants on New Year's Eve, when she'd been with Ben and purchased the world's sleaziest faux-leopard pants at the *Hustler* sex emporium on Sunset Boulevard, then worn them to the backlot party at Warner Brothers. The memory made her wince.

"What's wrong?" Susan asked. "Are they that bad?"

"No, they're great," she told her sister, trying to sound enthusiastic.

Susan laughed. She went to her nightstand for her cigarettes. "You're full of crap, Anna. You hate these pants. You're such a little prep girl."

"You used to be, too."

Susan torched her cigarette and took a long drag. "The difference is, it never really suited me." She regarded Anna thoughtfully. "Don't you ever do anything wrong, Anna? Don't you ever just want to break out and get crazy?"

"Does ten minutes in Noah's bungalow count?"

"Saving his sole, so to speak?" Susan grinned, replying with a rhetorical question. "Cammie filled me in on his, er, predilection. Anyway, that doesn't count."

"*Very* ick," Anna said, laughing. "And he seemed so normal!"

"You want normal, Anna, go out with the same boring preppie types you went out with back in New York. It's okay to go a little nuts, you know."

I did on New Year's Eve, Anna thought. *With Ben. And all I got for it was a broken heart.*

Anna tried to make light of Susan's remark. "So you think I should have let Noah slime my toes?"

"Hardly. You know what I mean."

Suddenly Anna wanted to tell Susan about Ben—she remembered a time when the two sisters had had no secrets from each other. Besides, hadn't Susan done many stupid and crazy things in her life? She'd be the first one to admit that. Why was it better to keep silent and let Susan believe that it was only the older sister who'd use bad judgment? They went back to the table to eat, and Anna took the plunge: she told Susan all about Ben.

"Wow. Who woulda thunk it?" Susan said. She lit another cigarette and tossed the match onto an uneaten crab cake. "That sucks, sweetie."

"Live and learn, I guess."

"Guys can be such shits."

Anna sighed. "Yeah."

Susan pulled her legs up and sat Indian-style at the table—a habit that Anna remembered from when they were kids.

"Mom hated it when you sat like that," Anna recalled. "She said it wasn't ladylike."

"Mom's seven thousand miles away; I think it's unlikely she's gonna find out. That is, unless you tell her."

"I don't tell her anything."

"Good. Anyway, Anna, how do you know this guy Ben isn't telling the truth? About why he split that night, I mean?"

"Sooz, come on. He abandoned me at three in the morning because he had to go save the life of some mystery celebrity girl. Does that strike you as plausible?"

Susan reached for a glass of ice water and drained it before she spoke. "No. Which is exactly what makes me think he could be telling the truth. I mean, from what you said, the guy is smart, right? Smart, smooth, hot. A guy like that could definitely make up a better lie."

Anna shook her head. "I sincerely doubt it."

"Take it from me. Ben could be telling you the truth."

Anna went to the open window, though there was nothing to see outside except a few lights along the walkway through the bungalows. She could smell jasmine and orange blossoms, flowers that bloomed year-round in Los Angeles, and inhaled deeply, trying to calm herself down. Why, why, why did it always come back to Ben? The image of him and his new girlfriend flooded her brain again. She so desperately wanted not to care!

"It doesn't matter anymore," she finally said, then turned back to her sister. "I'm over him. He's seeing someone else. And so am I."

Susan laughed. "Liar."

"I am! I was just with him, in fact. All afternoon. His name is Adam. He's the anti-Ben."

"I didn't mean that you're lying about seeing someone else, sweetie," Susan explained. "I meant that you're lying about being over Ben."

Anna felt her neck flush; she hoped that Susan couldn't see. "No, I'm not."

"Bull. I can smell the sexual tension clear across the room. You seriously need to get laid. I'm telling you, we should go partying with Cammie and Dee this weekend. Your assignment is to pick the hottest guy you meet and jump his bones."

When Susan got like this, it made Anna crazy. "First of all, that is terrible advice," Anna snapped. "Second of all, I told you, I'm going to a spa with Sam this weekend. I'm working on a screenplay for a short film, remember? And you were going with me—unless you've changed your mind. Third of all, Cammie and Dee are not high on my people-I-want-to-spend-my-precious-time-on-earth-with list. And fourth of all, meaningless sex is just so . . . so meaningless!"

"How would you know?" Susan asked laconically. "You've never had it."

"I don't need to have it to know."

"There's only one reason you'd say that, Anna. Because you already know the one guy it would be meaningful with."

Okay, now Susan was making her *really* nuts.

"If you mean Ben, you're wrong," Anna insisted. "Did your new best friend Cammie happen to mention that he used to be her boyfriend?"

"No." Susan seemed to falter a beat, which Anna found satisfying. "Really?"

"And did your other new best friend Dee Young happen to mention that she had a one-night stand with him?"

Susan's jaw dropped. "Are you serious?"

"Unfortunately, yes."

"What an asshole. I take back everything I said. The boy is a player."

"Thank you."

"But this other guy . . . what's his name?"

"Adam."

"Adam," Susan repeated. "What do you like about him?"

Anna thought long and hard. "He's nice," she said finally.

"Nice?" Susan hooted. "Nice? A new kitten is nice. Your third-grade teacher was nice. That guy you went to the ninth-grade prom with? Paul Brody, the one who looked like an albino, whose parents own half of the Upper East Side? He was nice. But you told me he drooled when he kissed. Anna, you're almost eighteen years old. You don't need nice!"

"Please, that's such a cliché," Anna insisted. "A guy can be hot without being a bad boy. Adam is terrific. He's smart. He's honest—"

"He'd make an excellent social worker, then," Susan opined. "Maybe there's an opening for him at Hazelden. But as a boyfriend? You'll be bored to death within three months. And that's why you came out here, isn't it? You don't need to be bored to death anymore!"

"Fine," Anna shot back. "And you don't need to go club hopping with Ben's former flames."

Susan looked defiant. "What do you expect me to do, Anna, never party again?"

"It's not like eating and sleeping, Susan. It's not something you *have* to do."

"Sorry. Once again your older sister is going to disappoint you."

Anna sighed. Sometimes Susan simply exhausted her. "Fine. Do whatever you want."

"You say it, but you don't mean it," Susan said.

"That's right. Because I love you. And I'd prefer it if you stuck around for the next fifty or sixty years."

Susan looked away. She was quiet for a long time. "Okay," she finally said. "You win. Forget Cammie and Dee. I'll come to Palm Springs with you."

"Great." Anna could feel her shoulders unhinging from her earlobes. At least she wouldn't have to worry about Susan for a few more days. She went to her sister and gave her a quick hug. "We'll have fun. You'll see."

Susan tugged on a lock of Anna's hair. "Probably not. But I know you're just looking out for me. Can I tell you something, though?"

"Sure."

"Think about what I said. You can't talk yourself into lusting after someone. And that quiet, steady kind of love—that can wait until middle-age spread sets in."

All the way home Anna did think about what Susan had said. Was she choosing safety over passion, and was she doing it because Ben had hurt her so badly?

She liked Adam. A lot. And she *was* attracted to him. But Susan was right: Anna didn't dream about ripping Adam's clothes off. Little people didn't bungee jump in her stomach when she thought of him. And no amount of liking him was going to make that happen. Whether it was because she was afraid or just because the chemistry wasn't there, she didn't know. But she did know this: it wasn't fair to Adam.

The question was, What the hell was she going to do about it?

But . . .

"*Limerence* is the early state of love or lust where one person sees another as perfect," Mrs. Breckner explained. "Basically, we're talking about lust. Gatsby lusted after Daisy but called it love. The difference between the two is—"

Mrs. Breckner's lecture was cut short by the bell. Anna sighed. Actually, she would have been interested in hearing what her teacher thought the difference between those two things was. She'd been up all night, tossing and turning, trying to figure out what, if anything, she should say to Adam. Maybe all she felt for Ben was lust, and it was coloring her judgment.

She dropped her notebook into her backpack and slung it over one shoulder, then exited the classroom with everyone else. Adam was leaning against the lockers just outside the door. She'd been avoiding him all day.

"Hey, stranger," he said, and gave her that sweet crooked smile. He fell in next to her and they headed down the hall. "Long time no see and all that. So, what's up?"

"Not much." Anna had a hard time making eye contact with him. "Want a ride home?"

"Yeah, sure." He held the door open for her. It was a rare overcast, gloomy afternoon. Adam furrowed his brow. "Hey, are you all right?"

"Yes. I've got a lot on my mind." She could hear how tense she sounded, how stilted.

It wasn't until they were inside her car that he spoke again. She was about to turn the key in the ignition when he put his hand over hers to stop her. "It doesn't take a mind reader to figure out that something is up with you, Anna. If it has something to do with me . . ."

Anna stared at her hands in her lap. This was horrible. More horrible than she had even imagined it would be.

"Oh, crap, it *does* have something to do with me," Adam said. He rubbed the star tattoo behind his ear.

"You know how much I like you, Adam." Anna's voice was low and earnest. She forced herself to look at him. "You're one of the greatest guys I've ever met."

"There's a big-ass 'but' coming, isn't there?" Adam guessed. "Something like, 'but Ben and I got back together.'"

"No. We didn't."

"Whew," Adam exhaled. "So what is it, then?"

"I don't . . . I'm not . . ." Anna couldn't figure out a way to say this without hurting Adam, which was the last thing in the world she wanted to do. "I feel very confused about guys at the moment," she finally said. "I just don't think I can have a relationship right now."

"If I was going too fast—"

"It's not that," Anna assured him. "I'm the one who kissed you, remember? I just think I need some time on my own. I care about you. A lot. And I don't want to hurt you . . ."

"Wait, you're breaking up with me so that you won't *hurt* me?" Adam asked. "That's not exactly logical."

"Yeah," Anna agreed. She rubbed one finger across the steering wheel. "I am doing a terrible job of this. Ben . . . hurt me. I'm not going to pretend he didn't. I was an idiot to let him hurt me, but . . . it happened. And I think I need to get over that, and learn some things about myself, before I get into another relationship. Does that make any sense at all?"

"Not really." Adam leaned his head back against the car door. "Damn! I mean, I know I should just say, 'Okay, cool, take all the time you need,' but frankly, that's not how I feel. It's not like we jumped into some hot and heavy—"

"I know that. I just need some time alone. I'll go to the desert with Sam this weekend and try to sort things out in my head."

"And how long will it take for you to 'sort things out in your head'?"

"I don't know, okay?" Anna heard the sharpness of her tone. She hadn't expected Adam to push her like this. "At the moment I'm terrible girlfriend material, Adam. And that isn't fair to either one of us."

Adam held his palms up. "What can I say?"

"I'm so sorry," Anna said, meaning it with all her heart. "I really do care about you. Maybe in the future—"

"What am I supposed to do, wait around for your call?"

"No. You should find a girl who deserves you. Because you are terrific."

"Yeah, great," Adam muttered. "This is the world's nicest kiss-off." He ran a hand over his stubbly hair. "Do what you need to do, then."

Anna nodded and started the car. She pulled out of the parking lot. In silence they headed for Adam's house. When she reached his driveway, he turned to her.

"I'm not exactly proud of how I handled that, Anna. If you need some time alone, then you need some time alone."

She felt like hugging him, he was such a sweetheart. Why couldn't she be madly in love with him? Why was her damn heart so utterly screwed up? "Thanks," she said. "For understanding."

"So I'll take a lot of cold showers and we'll see what happens down the road." Adam got out of the car and came around to the driver's side. He spoke with Anna through the open window. "Bowser is going to take this hard, you know."

Anna nodded. It was all she could manage. Adam gave her a half salute and she backed the car down the driveway. Adam was still watching her when she drove away. If she'd imagined that she'd feel better after breaking up with Adam, she'd imagined wrong. Because now she felt worse than ever. Why did girls seem to obsess about guys so much more than guys obsessed about girls? Anna need to take her mind off Adam and Ben entirely and replace it with something that was about *her* instead of about *them*.

She made a snap decision and turned right on Sunset Boulevard instead of left, which led to her father's house. She headed for the Beverly Hills Public Library. Research on her Gatsby script was just the thing to do, she decided. Maybe there were some essays on love and lust and limerence in *Gatsby* that would help her write her screenplay. She would simply throw herself into that project. Maybe it would turn out that she was a fabulous writer. She certainly knew enough about the subjects of life, love, lust, and limerence to do justice to a ten-minute film. At least when she was writing, she was in charge of what all the characters said and did.

She'd just have to write herself her own happy ending.

Sloppy Thirds

S am Sharpe pawed through her closet—actually, an entire room off her bedroom suite—trying to decide what to take to the spa. The key was to find a bathing suit that accentuated the positive. And eliminated the negative.

She had a black one from Calvin Klein with a small flounce at the bottom. It was great for covering up her thighs, but with the metal detailing, it made her look like Barbarella. There was always the less-is-more approach—sometimes showing more skin created an optical illusion. By diverting everyone's attention to the boobage, the flaws were often overlooked. *Crap!* It was already four o'clock, and she'd told Anna she'd pick her up at four-thirty to drive out to Palm Springs. With any luck, they'd beat the worst of the afternoon rush-hour traffic.

What to wear, what to wear, what to wear? It was unlikely that there'd be any hot young single guys at Veronique's. Yes, there were the Indian casinos in Palm Springs and lots of golf courses. Casinos plus golf equaled men. But Sam hated golfers—the clothes alone were enough to make you gag—and the casinos were strictly low-rent compared to, say, the Bellagio in Las Vegas. Low-rent casinos attracted low-rent men, and Sam had no interest in low-rent men. Or women.

Or *women?* What the hell made *that* little thought jump into her head? But she knew the answer—the four-letter *A* word. *Anna.* Okay. So she had a crush. It was cute, really. If little girls could get crushes on girls, then big girls could get crushes on girls. It didn't *mean* anything.

As if to prove the point, she wrote a mental to-do list of hot guys. Well, there was Ben, of course, her first love. And then there was . . . um . . . let's see. The Pinelli brothers. They were both coming out to V's on Saturday morning to help with the film. Monty wasn't her type, but Parker was serious eye candy. Still, Sam suspected that he loved himself too much to give anyone else equal time.

There had to be someone besides Ben. But weirdly, no one came to mind. She'd much rather give Anna a massage than have some sweaty, hairy guy she'd meet in the sauna try to stick his tongue in her ear and—

Oh, shit. *She'd rather give Anna a massage?*

She knew she had to get her mind on something else, so she concentrated on her packing. She tracked down the one swimsuit that she liked, by Gottex, plus jeans, shorts, and a selection of Versace and Pucci T-shirts, and threw it all into the ice-blue leather Coach suitcase on her bed. Underwear, too. As she struggled with the zipper, her bedside phone rang.

"Yuh?" she answered.

"Hi, Sam, it's Anna."

"Hi, Anna," Sam said, careful to keep her tone breezy. "What's up?"

"I'm at my sister's bungalow at the Beverly Hills Hotel. So you won't need to pick me up at my father's house. We can meet you in the lobby."

"Okay."

"Are you sure you don't want to use two cars? Because it's not a problem. We can take Susan's Mustang."

"Nah. Monty and Parker will schlep all of the equipment in the van. It'll be more fun for us all to drive out together. So, see you in a few."

"Sam? I finished the script. I was up most of the night working on it."

"Great." Sam tried to sound enthusiastic. "When do I get to see it? You really should have sent it to me for notes."

"I can read it to you in the car on the way, if you want."

"I'll just read it myself when we get there. Anyway, look for me in, like, half an hour."

Sam hung up, nibbling at her lower lip. It was one thing to have a little crushette on Anna and quite another to become a cheerleader for her new screenwriting career. Every studio exec in Hollywood tried to make his bimbo girlfriend into a screenwriter or producer. It was pathetic. Well, Sam had penned her own backup script just in case. It hadn't been hard. Rather than tell a complete story—hard to do in just ten minutes—it had occurred to her to do the whole thing in the style of an *Entertainment Tonight* fawning television feature on a Jay Gatsby–like character but with a shocking, Richard-Cory-put-a-bullet-through-his-head-like reveal at the ending. Edwin Arlington Robinson himself would have been proud. Yes, Sam would give Anna's script a listen. She hoped it was good. But chances were, it wouldn't be.

Sam finished packing, loaded her suitcases into her dad's Cherokee, and headed to the hotel to pick up Anna and her sister. The traffic was manageable for once, so she got there at four-thirty, as advertised. Anna and Susan were waiting in front with their suitcases by the bellman's stand, which gave Sam a chance to check out Susan as she pulled up. Cammie had told Sam all about Susan, of course. According to Cammie, Anna's sister, Susan, was the poster girl for Party Hearty and had been in rehab more times than Whitney Houston. She certainly looked the part, in an artfully ripped black T-shirt, low-riding camouflage pants, and a black leather motorcycle jacket. She wore red lipstick and a lot of black eyeliner and bore a passing resemblance to Marilyn Monroe.

So evidently Anna's big sis was going for a sexbomb thing. It was working.

As the bellman loaded the bags into the back of Sam's Jeep, Anna introduced Sam to Susan. Susan offered Sam her hand. "Nice to meet you," she said in perfectly modulated, cultured tones that were at odds with her tough-girl appearance.

Funny, Sam thought. *You can take the girl out of the Upper East Side of Manhattan, but you can't take the Upper East Side out of the girl.* Or put it into the girl, for that matter, if she didn't have it. Some people tried, of course. But Susan and Anna were the real thing.

Anna got in the front, Susan in the back, and Sam pulled onto Sunset Boulevard. As they headed toward the 101 freeway, Sam asked Susan whether she'd be interested in helping with the film.

"Some school thing?" Susan asked disdainfully. "Definitely not."

Sam was taken aback. Who the hell was Susan to dismiss it as some school thing? The person doing the "school thing" was in the process of becoming a really famous filmmaker. Besides—hel-*lo*—she was Jackson Sharpe's daughter.

"Actually—is it Susan?" Sam called into the backseat. "A short of mine was on IFC last year, Susan," Sam said. "Maybe Anna mentioned that my father is Jackson Sharpe. He watches all my reels. So you never know."

"I love your dad," Susan said. "Especially in *The Last Patriot.* I think I've seen all of his movies."

Ah, yes. Drop the magic name of Jackson Sharpe, and they always come running.

"Thanks," Sam said, eyeing Susan in the rearview mirror. "So, changed your mind?"

"God, no."

No? Sam wasn't used to "no." Usually everyone she asked to be in one of her films said yes. Even girls who hated her said yes. It was like some kind of Los Angeles disease, where everyone thought they were one break away from becoming a star. But Susan Percy couldn't care less. And now, Sam could see in the rearview mirror that Susan was underscoring her refusal by leaning back and closing her eyes.

Well, to hell with that, Sam thought, eyeing Susan's I-wish-it-was-1977-and-I-was-dating-a-Sex-Pistol look. What music would annoy this girl the most? She rooted around under her feet for a CD, found an old Frank Sinatra disc that her father adored and she detested, and popped it in. The familiar repeating five-note intro to "New York, New York" blasted through the Cherokee.

Sam checked the rearview mirror. Susan's eyes opened for the briefest second, then closed again.

Touché.

Actually, this was a Sinatra song that Sam actually liked. At Ben's bar mitzvah the band had played this song, and Ben had danced with her to it. It was a nice memory.

"You like this music?" she asked Anna.

"Not much," Anna admitted.

"It's my dad's," Sam confided. "My pubescent step-mother likes to sing to him. It's aural torture. You know how the Pop-Tart got her start in the business?"

"No."

Sam changed lanes—they were approaching the free-way entrance—then turned the music down. "She was a junior at Santa Monica College, and some guy saw her running on the median of San Vicente Boulevard and told her she could be a star. She moved in with him, and he cast her as a runaway in *Against Their Will* for Showtime."

Sam glanced at Anna, who looked completely preoc-cupied, then back at the road. She realized that she'd been babbling as nervously as if the two of them were on a first date. "I have no idea why I'm telling you this. It's boring, I know."

"Sorry," Anna said. "I was just thinking about this party I have to attend late Sunday afternoon for my internship at Apex. I'm supposed to take a new client of theirs."

"The Steinberg thing? I know all about it. I'll be there, too," Sam said.

"What an incestuous little world this is," Anna com-mented.

"Like it's any different where you come from. Same turds, different bowl."

"You're right," Anna acknowledged. She turned toward her sister in the backseat. "You're coming to the party with me tomorrow, right?"

"I'm still suffering through the fact that the preten-tious little twit got famous," Susan said without open-ing her eyes. "God, he used to wheeze when he kissed me. Talk about gross."

"I'll take that as a yes," Anna said.

Sam wanted to continue the discussion, but Anna closed her eyes. A few minutes later she was asleep. She looked so calm and peaceful that Sam couldn't bear to interrupt her slumber. So she just shut up and drove.

To Anna, the three-hour drive to the desert seemed endless. She mostly dozed fitfully, wondering if she'd done the right thing by calling a halt to things with Adam. She could still see the hurt on his face. Susan slept through most of the ride, and Sam listened to music that Anna really didn't like. But they'd finally reached the outskirts of Palm Springs and were driving between the two huge expanses of power-generating windmills that spread out along both sides of the freeway. There were hundreds of them, illuminated by floodlights, spinning madly in the gusty desert wind. Interspersed were billboards for Indian casinos.

"Casino Morongo." From the backseat a just-awakened Susan read one of the billboards aloud. "We should blow the spa tomorrow night and hit it."

Anna tensed. *Here we go again.*

"That's not really a good idea, Sooz."

"Jeez, Anna, I can drink Red Bull or something. I just got out of rehab," Susan added for Sam's benefit.

Anna wished Susan had kept that last comment to herself. There was a time when Susan was even more private than Anna.

"What's the biggie?" Sam asked, noticing Anna's reaction. "Half the people I know are in rehab. The other half just got out." She checked her side-view mirror and then shifted smoothly into the passing lane.

An exaggeration, obviously, but Anna thought it was kind of Sam to take such a sanguine attitude.

"Tell me about it," Susan agreed. "So, you up for some fast dice and fast boys, Sam?"

Sam's eyes flicked to Anna, then back to the road. She sensed Anna's discomfort over her sister being in such an alcohol-soaked environment as a casino. "You know, Susan, let's just hang at the spa. People kill to get a reservation at V's. You should take advantage of it. And the massages are awesome."

"You can get a good massage anywhere." Susan leaned forward and tugged on a lock of Anna's hair. "Come on. Let's have fun. It'll help you get Flower Boy out of your system."

Anna's stomach clutched. Too late, she realized she should have told her sister not to mention anything about Ben or Adam to Sam—that Sam seemed to be oddly obsessed with Anna's love life.

In the old days she could have counted on Susan's discretion. These days discretion wasn't even in her sister's vocabulary.

"Flower Boy?" Sam echoed.

"Yeah, it's wild," Susan told Sam. "The guy sent Anna hundreds of roses."

"Adam Flood?" Sam guessed.

"Ben something," Susan filled in. "I hear he's an ass."

"*Ben?*" Sam echoed, incredulous. She took her eyes

off the road and looked at Anna. "I thought you guys were done. He sent you flowers from Princeton?"

"Um . . . he might still be in Los Angeles," Anna murmured, trying desperately to think of a way to change the subject without being obvious.

Sam gripped the wheel tightly now and stared straight ahead. "I guess he wants you back."

Anna shrugged. Sam seemed really intense about this, and she had no idea why. Was it just on behalf of Cammie? She decided to change the subject. "Let's talk about our film, okay? I can read it to you—"

"Anna was smart to blow this guy off," Susan plunged on, seemingly oblivious to her sister's discomfort or maybe because of it. "Players are such shits."

"Yeah," Sam echoed. "You were right to blow him off."

But . . . wasn't it only yesterday that Sam was saying what a great guy Ben is? Anna thought about reminding Sam of this. But she didn't. "If you two don't mind, I'd really rather not talk about him. Or Adam. Or any other guy, for that matter."

Susan laughed. "That's a joke, right?"

"No. I'm serious. Right now, I'm not all that interested in guys."

Sam's heart nearly skipped a beat. *Anna wasn't all that interested in guys?* Was she trying to send Sam some kind of signal? Or was that just Sam's fevered imagination? And even if she was sending a signal, Sam wasn't exactly sure what she was supposed to do about it. Sam had never really given the next step much thought. Would she have to get Anna alone in a dark corner and make a move? The idea of it was almost too weird to even think about.

Sam was getting way ahead of herself. What she needed was more information. "So what *are* you interested in, then?" Sam asked, as casually as possible.

"Our film," Anna told her. "And me. For a change."

Oh. So that was what she meant. Sam smiled in relief. She wasn't quite ready to go *there*. Yet.

"Sounds good to me."

Susan nodded. "Mind if I smoke?" she asked Sam.

"It's your lungs," Sam told her.

Susan stuck a cigarette between her lips, torched it, and cracked open her window. "Sloppy thirds is a nasty concept, even to me."

Sam swerved, nearly running onto the shoulder. "*What* did you just say?"

"I don't blame Anna," Susan said, making a face and exhaling a smoke ring. "Who wants to be someone's leftovers? First came Cammie, then came Dee."

Sam blanched. Dee clearly had never mentioned a hookup with Ben.

"Dee? No way. I can't believe Ben would . . . How could he . . . ? And then to send you enough flowers to cover the Tournament of Roses parade . . ."

"Ben's . . ." Anna stopped. She was about to tell Sam what happened with her and Ben on New Year's Eve. But she'd already talked about it with Susan. Did she have to involve Sam? Look who Sam considered her nearest and dearest—Cammie Sheppard, a girl Anna was pretty sure would stab you in the heart and laugh while you bled just for giggles. Talk about your heart of darkness.

And yet, Anna really wanted a friend in Los Angeles. She *needed* a friend in Los Angeles. Sam was the only candidate for the position. Anna thought about her life-long friendship with Cyn back in New York. Cyn definitely had friends Anna couldn't abide, but Anna didn't hold that against her. Why hold Sam to a different standard?

"Yo?" Sam prompted.

"Oh, just tell her," Susan said. "I realize our parents are the king and queen of Keep Your Mouth Shut at All Times, but it's not like either one of them is happy."

Maybe Susan is right, Anna thought. *Besides, I didn't do anything horrible.*

"Sam," Anna began. "I'd appreciate it if you didn't tell Dee and Cammie what I'm about to tell you."

Sam laughed. "I don't talk to them about what's really going on in my life, much less yours."

So Anna filled Sam in, right down to Ben's ridiculous excuse about how he'd abandoned Anna to save some mystery celebrity actress friend's life. "And that," she concluded, "is the whole sordid little tale."

Actually, it wasn't. She'd left out the details about what had—or hadn't—happened belowdecks on the boat right after the stroke of midnight. The status of her virginity was one thing that was going to remain private.

"Jeez," Sam breathed. "That's a movie."

"I know Ben is a friend of yours, Sam. But maybe you don't know him as well as you thought you did. My theory is, he only wants me back because I walked away."

Sam looked pensive. "Maybe."

"Maybe?" Anna echoed. "You don't actually buy his story, do you?"

"Well, he knows a lot of actresses," Sam said as the heart of Palm Springs finally loomed in the distance. "Half the girls on the WB went to Beverly Hills High."

Susan scooched forward in her seat. "So who's he friends with?"

"Let me think. . . ." Sam nibbled at her lower lip. "We went to a House of Blues Christmas party last year and he left with that chick who's on *Smallville*, what's-her-name."

"Sorry, I don't watch much TV," Anna said.

"Right. I'm trying to think who else . . . ," Sam mused.

"Someone no one would believe is an addict," Susan put in eagerly.

Anna couldn't believe it. Her sister had been at the princess of Jarudi's eighteenth birthday party because the queen had gone to boarding school with their mother. She'd sat in the royal box at Wimbledon. And now Susan was playing guess-Ben's-mystery-celebrity-addict-wench?

Maybe it was something in the West Coast water.

"Okay. Not too many people know this," Sam began, her voice low despite the fact that there were only the three of them in the car. "But after Ben and Cammie broke up, a certain very famous actress—she's been on a sitcom everyone has watched *forever* and is married to a certain very famous actor . . . he's to die for—met Ben at a party. She'd had a fight with her husband because she thought he was smoking pot, so she came to the party without him. She didn't know Ben was still in high school. One thing led to another—"

"How do you know all this?" Susan asked.

"For God's sake, Susan, it was *my* party. And the same people will be at the Steinbergs' party. Can you imagine if she's all over Brad's case for smoking dope when she's the one with the problem?" Sam asked.

"Brad?" Susan echoed. "Did you say Brad? As in Brad—?"

"Hold it. *Stop right there,*" Sam insisted. "I never dish about my friends. I only dish about other people's friends."

The conversation continued in this vein. Anna didn't participate, but she did, admittedly, listen. And wonder. What if Sam was right? What if Ben really had told her the truth?

No. It didn't matter anymore.

Yes, it does, said a nagging little voice in the back of her head, *because when you fell asleep before, you were dreaming about him.*

Me-Me-Me-Whine-Whine-Whine

V's had no sign, but Sam knew where to find the private road. Tiny white lights flickered in the cactus along the sides of the gravel entrance. It was the first indication of any civilization. Then she rounded a tight bend and pulled to a stop at a guardhouse. A burly man in a khaki uniform stepped out. There was nothing to identify this as the entrance to Veronique's spa. In fact, Anna thought it looked more like an entrance to a right-wing militia retreat.

"Good evening, ladies," he said. "Name, please?"

"Sam Sharpe," Sam told him.

"One moment please, Miss Sharpe." The guy in khaki stepped back into the guardhouse and typed furiously into a computer, then stepped out of the guardhouse again. "You're expected, Miss Sharpe."

He pressed a button on his beeper. Suddenly the road past the guardhouse was illuminated in breathtaking white and orange light, and a gate blocking their path opened automatically. Two minutes later they reached a grand columned building that looked something like the

White House. Three gorgeous young men in khakis and
aquamarine golf shirts sprang to action, opening doors
and taking their luggage out of the back of the
Cherokee. "Miss Sharpe, Miss Percy, and Miss Percy,
welcome to Veronique's," said the oldest of them, who
had cheekbones that could cut ice. "We'll bring these
bags to your suites. Miss Sharpe, here are your key
cards."

The valet handed Sam the key cards for their suites.

"No check-in?" Anna asked Sam.

"V keeps a file on all their guests and preps the valet.
Check-in was all taken care of by phone. And don't tip.
It's tacked on to the bill."

Anna stretched, stiff from the long ride, amazed at
how chilly it was—the temperature couldn't have been
higher than forty-five degrees. Then she remembered
that they were in the desert in January.

"Okay, you're all set," the valet promised. "Go
inside and warm up. And don't worry, forecast is for
temps in the seventies tomorrow."

The three girls stepped into the spacious lobby. The air
was warm, the lights muted. The colors in the wild-orchid
centerpiece picked up the pale lavenders and pinks from
the inlaid marble-and-limestone floor. Priceless art
adorned the walls—Anna recognized a Monet, a Titian,
and an El Greco. In lieu of an actual registration counter,
there was a pair of desks with discreet signs that simply
said "Guest Assistance." Behind the desk, there was a
massive oil painting of a woman who had to be Veronique

herself. She bore a strong resemblance to Donald Trump's ex-wife.

Susan looped an arm through Anna's as they crossed the lobby toward a door that led to their suites. "Ah, the life of the young and idle rich. Aren't we the lucky ones."

"We are, actually," Anna replied.

"I know that. I really do." Susan squeezed Anna's hand. "When I get in a me-me-me-whine-whine-whine loop, just smack me across the face, okay?"

"And you do the same for me," Anna said, hugging her sister. "This is going to be fun, Sooz. We haven't spent a weekend together in a long time."

"Miss Sharpe?" A Scandinavian-accented voice made Anna turn around. A stunning blond woman in a perfectly cut simple blue dress came toward them.

"Ingrid!" Sam exclaimed. "How are you?"

"Happy to have you back with us, Miss Sharpe," she told Sam. Only the understated badge reading "Ingrid Svenson" and a simple *V* monogram gave away the fact that the young woman worked for the spa. "I'm sorry I didn't see you come in. Dinner is being served until ten in the Versailles Room, or you can dine en suite if you prefer. Miss Sharpe, you're in the Marilyn suite, Miss Anna Percy, you're in the Bette, and Miss Susan Percy, we've put you in the Rita." She gestured to the other end of the lobby. "Your suites are just beyond the patio and the pool, through those double doors. A short walk. Or I can ring for Paolo to bring the golf cart if you like."

Before any of the girls could respond, a female voice called, "Hey, you three!"

Cammie Sheppard.

Anna seethed. What the hell was Cammie Sheppard doing here? She noticed that Sam didn't look at all surprised. Cammie air-kissed Sam, then Susan. Anna, she ignored.

"This is great, Susan," Cammie exclaimed. "I didn't know you were coming."

"I didn't know you'd be here, either," Susan admitted.

Cammie wagged a playful finger at Sam. "Bad girl. You know you're supposed to tell me everything."

"Sam didn't happen to mention it to me, either," Anna observed, her tone flat.

Cammie's eyes flicked to Anna. She yawned. "Oh. Hi, Anna."

"When did you plan all this?" Anna asked Sam under her breath.

"Cammie and Dee and I booked weeks ago," Sam admitted.

"You could have told me."

"It's not like they're going to be in our way. We're here for business, they're here for pleasure."

"Is Dee here yet?" Anna asked.

As the double doors swung open, Dee's perky voice answered Anna's question. "Wow, hi, you guys! This is going to be so fun! What suites are you guys in? Want to go have dinner?"

Anna's head began to pound. "I need to unpack," she said. "And we need to go over my script, Sam."

"It doesn't have to be this very minute, does it?" Sam asked.

"Anna," Cammie sighed. "Can't you see we're making an effort? This our little way of saying we'd like to bond with you."

"I'm not really very hungry, so I'll see you all later. Susan? Want to come with me?"

Susan shrugged. "Honestly? I'm famished."

"Let's do dinner on the patio," Sam suggested. "Is that hot waiter from Denmark still here? What's his name?"

"Ulrik," Cammie filled in. "Yes, he's here, and he lives to serve. Day and night," she added knowingly. "He's on right now, in fact."

Susan turned to Anna. "You mind?"

Yes, Anna wanted to say. But it seemed so . . . petty. "Do whatever you want. It's fine."

"We'll go over the script later, Anna," Sam assured her.

"All right. I guess it's good this way. I'll have some extra time for last-minute rewrites," Anna added lamely since she wasn't sure what, if any, rewrites she needed to do. She excused herself and took the short walk past the pool until she reached a two-story building built in muted earth tones with an adobe exterior. The dozen suites in the building were listed in alphabetical order on a wooden sign; Anna saw that hers was on the first floor, closest to the mountains. She slid her access card into the front slot, then waited for the green light to blink so she could enter.

The living room was all white—plush carpet, velvet couch, and chair. A vase of white roses sat in the center

of the coffee table. Next to it was a white bowl full of
fresh fruit. Anna went into the bedroom. Over the white
canopy bed hung an oil painting of Bette Davis wearing a
white sarong.

Anna went into the bathroom, also all white. There
was a bathtub deep enough for swimming and large
enough for four, with a crystal bowl of rose petals to
float on the water should she want them. On the white
marble vanity was an array of miniature beauty prod-
ucts, perfumes and oils, shampoos and conditioners,
each in distinctive white packaging with a gold V. A
handwritten note addressed to Anna and signed by
Ingrid explained that these were compliments of
Veronique and that of course all of them were available
for purchase at the spa's gift shop. Or Anna could order
via the interactive television in her bedroom.

Anna washed her face with Veronique's complimen-
tary Gentle Glow Washing Emulsion. It smelled like
petunias and musk—too cloying for Anna's taste. Next
to the bed was a white leather binder with the familiar
V monogram. Anna opened it; it contained a detailed
description of the endless services that Veronique's
offered its guests. She came to the massage section—
thirty seconds in the presence of Cammie and Dee had
made her tense. A massage sounded great. There was
marine mineral hydromassage. Thai massage. Cedar oil
sports massage. Hot lava-rock massage. Ylang-ylang
massage with four hands. Four hands?

Anna unpacked and settled down on the couch to

brainstorm a title for her script. Just then there was a discreet knock on her door. When Anna opened it, Dee stood there, holding a bottle of champagne and two flutes. "Can I come in? " she asked.

Good breeding won out again, which was why Anna nodded.

Dee stepped in and looked around. "Wow, nice. I'm in Madonna. Madonna is very colorful. But Bette Davis is so soothing. Kind of virginal. You know, all white. Not that Bette Davis was a virgin. I mean, she was married and everything."

"I really don't know much about her," Anna said, unable to figure out why Dee was paying her a visit.

Dee gestured toward the couch. "Mind?"

"A few minutes, that's all," Anna said. "I'm a little tired. And I need to work on my—" She gestured toward the script on the coffee table.

"I know an herbalist who can tell why you're tired just by washing your hair," Dee said as she put the bottle and flutes on the white coffee table. "So, I'm here as kind of a peace offering."

"We're not at war, Dee."

"Yeah, but . . ." Dee blew the shaggy bangs off her forehead. "Sam didn't tell you we'd be here, right?" Anna went to sit in the wing chair.

"Right."

"We always come here after the holidays. You know, kind of to detox. Oh, speaking of detox, I hear your sister just got out of rehab. That's good."

Anna's head started to pound again. "I don't really want to discuss—"

"No, you're right, I'm sorry," Dee said quickly. "Do you know that Cammie pretended she'd been in rehab, too, so that your sister would feel better? Isn't that sweet?"

Anna had no idea that Dee knew about Susan. Not that she was surprised. On the other hand, knowing Dee, she could have been making it all up as easily as if it were true. "I doubt that Cammie has ever done anything sweet in her life, Dee."

"Deep down, she's very kind," Dee insisted. "But after her mother died, she turned very hard on the outside. Anyway, where was I? I kind of wanted to apologize. That we got sprung on you like this."

"It's not your fault. Sam should have told me."

"Yeah. She knows you hate our guts. I know you say you don't, but not admitting to anger is really toxic, so I wish you'd just, you know, say it. But I think we got off on the wrong foot. Especially now that you and Ben are history. Which is why I thought we could have a toast. To starting over."

"Shouldn't you be careful about drinking, Dee?" Anna asked pointedly.

"Oh, you mean—" Dee patted her stomach. She hoisted the bottle. "Sparkling cider. Alcohol-free." She popped the bottle, half filled the flutes, and handed one to Anna. "Here's to a new friendship."

Anna made a small toasting gesture, then took a sip

of the cider. "So . . . nice of you to stop by. But I'm sure the others will be missing you."

If Dee had read the mythical *This Is How We Do Things* Big Book, East Coast WASP edition, then she would have known that "I'm sure the others will be missing you" was code for "Please leave."

Unfortunately, Dee wasn't all that well-read.

She settled back into the couch cushions. "I'm not hungry anymore. I did a lymphatic drainage about an hour ago and it feels wrong to eat after that. You know, tomorrow you should think about doing the rebirthing session with me. It's so amazing. You go into this heated pool naked—"

"I'll be busy working on the film with Sam."

Dee's lower lip went out. "Oh. Okay. I just thought maybe we could be friends."

"Maybe we can, Dee. It takes time."

Dee nodded solemnly. "Gosh. What's it like to be you?"

Anna was taken aback. "Sorry?"

"I mean, you're so perfect. I just wonder what that's like."

"Dee, I'm not perfect."

"Yes, you are. You must have done something really great in a past life to luck out so much in this one. That's why Ben is with you and not me. Do you think you and Ben were together in a past life?"

"I have no idea."

"It could be." Dee sipped her sparkling cider. "That would explain everything. It's fate."

Anna put her champagne flute on the coffee table. "Dee. If you want to be my friend, can you at least be honest with me?"

"You mean about . . . ?" Dee put her hand on her stomach again. Then she looked away. "I don't want to talk about that."

"But you said you wanted to be friends." Anna decided to push it. If she had to sit here with this bizarre girl, she might at least attempt to clear some up some of the maddening puzzle. In some ways, her decision about Adam and Ben made it easier.

"I do."

"Ben told me he's not even sure if anything happened that night."

Dee's eyes grew into twin azure Frisbees. "He said that?"

"It's not that he doesn't care about your feelings, it's just that he drank too much that night and his memory isn't clear."

Tears filled Dee's eyes. "So it didn't mean anything?"

Okay, unless Ben was out-and-out lying, this girl was seriously off the wall.

"Maybe you built whatever happened between the two of you into something that it really wasn't."

Dee blinked rapidly. "You two are in love. I knew it."

"I'm *not* in love with him. It's over. Whatever 'it' was."

Dee sighed. "Your aura tells a different story. Well, all I have to say is, in my next life, I want to come back as you." She stood and walked slowly toward the door, the cider forgotten.

Beyond weird. Was Dee on something? If so, she needed to quit. And if not, then maybe she *should* be on something. As in, something prescribed by a psychiatrist. When Dee reached the door, she turned back. "Just tell him the baby and I won't need any financial support. But Ben Junior or little Delia will definitely need his emotional support." Then she closed the door behind her, leaving Anna staring at the placard that explained what to do in the event of a fire or an earthquake.

Well, that covered natural disasters, but what were people to do if they stepped into an alternate reality?

As Anna drew a hot bath, her imagination got the best of her. What if Dee was telling the truth? What if she *was* carrying Ben's child? Anna would never be able to look at that child without being reminded of Ben and all the hurt he'd caused her. What an awful burden for an innocent child to carry.

But as Anna added designer bubbles to her bath, she forced herself to dismiss those horrible thoughts. Once she lay in the oversized, sunken tub and lazily scattered the rose petals into the water, it was easy to let her thoughts wander off in a different direction. If ever there was a bathtub that screamed "tub for two," this was it. In some ways, she already missed Adam. She always felt great when she was with him. But that wasn't reason enough to lead him on when she was lusting after another boy.

No. Tub for one was definitely a better idea.

Honesty

Ben lay on a lounge chair by his parents' backyard pool, nursing a beer, staring at the murky, light-polluted Los Angeles night sky. It was nearly two o'clock in the morning, but he was unable to sleep. His father was missing in action and his mother couldn't stop crying. Home was a disaster. In fact, it felt like everything in his life was a disaster.

Where was Anna now? Was she looking up at the same stars right this minute? Did she think of him at all? Probably not, except to be glad to be rid of him. But even as he thought that, another part of him knew it wasn't true. It couldn't be true. He knew Adam Flood. Even liked him—they'd played pickup basketball together, and Adam had kicked his ass. Adam Flood was a good guy. But Ben was certain that Adam couldn't make her feel that way he could make her feel. If he could only talk to her once more and really explain—

Bullshit. She's got a new guy. You already decided to let her go, man. So give it a rest.

Ben was so startled when his cell phone rang that he nearly dropped his Heineken. "Hello?"

"Hi. I was dreaming about you." No one else in the world had that dusky, throaty voice.

"It's two o'clock in the morning, Cammie," Ben said wearily.

"No, really, I was," Cammie said.

"I don't want to know what."

"Yes, you do. We weren't even in bed."

"Well, that's surprising."

"Very funny. Listen: You were a lawyer, and you were arguing a case before the United States Supreme Court. I was in the gallery, watching you. And I was so proud."

Cammie's behavior was so out of character, Ben actually looked at the phone, as if he'd magically be able to look through it and see her. "That's . . . nice, Cammie," he said, since he couldn't come up with anything better.

"Yeah," she said wistfully. "It was."

Okay, something had to be up with Cammie. She was a calculating girl. Ben took a contemplative sip of his beer. "What do you want, Cammie?"

"Should I go for honesty?"

"Sure," Ben said.

"What I want is . . . a fresh start. For us."

"Come on, Cam," he gently chided her. "There is no 'us' anymore and you know it."

"There could be. Do you have any idea how sorry I am? That so many things went wrong?"

"I'm sorry, too, Cammie, but—"

"Is this because of Anna?" Cammie asked.

"We broke up long before I even met her, Cam."

"But why?" Cammie wailed.

Ben could hear the tears in her voice. It was so unlike the ice queen that he knew Cammie to be. This tender, vulnerable side was one she kept well hidden. Which made it much more difficult to tell her that it was really over, forever. "We both moved on, Cammie," he finally said.

"But if you hadn't fallen for Anna, we would have gotten together again at Jackson's wedding. I just know it."

"Is that why you tore off half of Anna's dress that night?"

"If I didn't want you, I never would have done that. You should take it as a compliment. We really have to talk, Ben. In person. So why don't you come up here?"

"Up where?"

"I'm at Veronique's spa. You know, in Palm Springs. We can go hiking in the desert. Or put up the Do Not Disturb sign and stay in bed all day. I know everything you love, Ben. I know exactly how to kish you. . . ."

Cammie was slurring. That explained everything.

"Cammie, have you been drinking?"

"A little wine, that's all."

Ben took another swallow of his beer. "Cammie, I really do appreciate the offer, but—"

"Would you come if Anna was here?"

That got Ben's attention. "Is she?"

"No," Cammie said quickly. "She isn't."

"It doesn't matter," Ben said sadly. "She blew me

off. I did some stupid things. I'm getting what I deserve."

"What stupid things? Like what happened on New Year's Eve?"

Ben winced. "How do you know about that?"

"Like there are any secrets in Beverly Hills. I know who the girl was, by the way."

"*What* girl?"

"The one you dumped Anna for on New Year's Eve. She'd *love* to know."

"Cammie—"

"*L-o-v-e* is the name, isn't it? You met her at your mom's fund-raiser last summer for Cedars-Sinai. You told me all about it, remember? Her pure-as-the-driven-snow public image and her nasty private habits. The lines she did off the cover of her first CD. How wasted she got when her movie tanked. You said she was the Wacko from Waco."

"I did not, Cammie."

"Ben, tell me the truth. When we were together, were you cheating on me with her?"

"Come on, cut it out."

Ben stood and walked over to the swimming pool. He was barefoot, so he sat on the edge and dangled his feet into the heated water. "First of all, I never said any of those things about her. And I never slept with her. We're friends, that's all."

"That's Beverly Hills code for 'I fucked her brains out but I'm being discreet.'"

"Cammie, you can think whatever you want; I didn't sleep with her."

Ben heard Cammie sigh. "It would have been easier if you had. Then at least I'd understand why you broke up with me. Come on, Ben." Her voice was low, sexy, hypnotizing. "Come out to the desert. It's a glorious night out here."

For one instant Ben was tempted by the head below his waist. From a purely physical point of view, there'd never been anyone like Cammie. A night with her could potentially dull the pain he was feeling over Anna.

But no. That would just be one more mistake piled atop a tower of them. "I'm sorry, Cammie. I can't give you what you want."

He heard her sob—something he'd never heard from her before—then she clicked off. *Sheesh.* He dove into the pool, then surfaced and floated on his back, trying to pick out a constellation—any constellation—in the night sky. He looked for a long, long time. But what he was searching for couldn't be found in the stars.

A Scientific Fact

As the ochre light of morning streamed through her window, Anna read over the new pages of her screenplay. She'd been up all night revising and had come up with the perfect title: *Three-Way*. The rewrite was a massive improvement, but she still didn't know whether what she'd written was any good.

The three characters were now renamed: the girl was Nina, and the guys were Dan and Mike.

After having wrestled forever with the dialogue— and deciding at three in the morning that her characters spoke as if they'd stepped out of a Harlequin romance— Anna had finally elected to write three intercuttable monologues where her characters talked directly to the camera.

Dan's family had recently made a ton of money in the stock market; Mike came from an elite Boston Brahmin family. As for Nina, Anna decided to have her focus on who she was and what she wanted instead of on her background. And in classic Gatsbyan tradition, these hopes and dreams would be in direct conflict to each other: to want a big family and a big career, a simple life and a lot of money, to live a long life but one that involved taking physical risks, and so on.

The three monologues could also be used as voice-overs to the footage that they would shoot.

It probably sucks, Anna thought as she stood. Time to face Sam. She'd delivered a copy to her early that morning; they'd agreed to meet on the patio at eleven to talk about it.

When Anna reached the dining room's outdoor patio, Sam was already at a table in the sun, drinking a steaming cup of what she told Anna was Flora BIJA Healing Tea. She wore a stretch Pucci T-shirt in a riot of primary colors and Seven jeans. Her makeup was as perfectly applied as always, and it was obvious that she'd had her hair blown out that morning at the spa salon.

A waiter appeared almost instantly. Anna ordered a lemonade as Sam reported that Susan had gone somewhere with Cammie and that Dee was taking a yoga class.

"Parker's here already," Sam said, indicating the outdoor bar. Anna saw him there with a well-preserved middle-aged woman who wore a pink hibiscus behind one ear. Its shocking-pink color matched a fuzzy sweater so small that it made her breasts look like lethal weapons.

"Too bad we're not getting that on film," Sam said as the older woman edged closer to Parker with barely disguised lust in her eyes. "Chick's a classic: grew up in Simi Valley . . . married some TV industry schlub . . . rode his gravy train all the way here."

Anna glanced down at her screenplay—it was on the table, next to Sam's teacup. Sam was talking about everything but it. Not a good sign.

Anna tapped a finger against the title page. "Do you hate it?"

Sam smiled behind her Gucci aviator sunglasses. "You're nervous! I don't think I've ever seen you nervous."

"Well, enjoy the moment." Anna folded her arms. "So?"

"Okay, okay. What you wrote is good."

Anna was amazed at how pleased she was at the compliment. "Really?"

"Not great," Sam cautioned. "We'll make some last-minute dialogue changes before we shoot, of course. But I already gave Parker the Dan monologue to work on, so that says something. See that guy talking with Monty up at the bar? With the square jaw and the crew cut? That's Jamie Cresswell. I think his ancestors came over on the *Mayflower* or something."

"How do you know?"

"Because he told me this morning over egg-white omelets. He's never done any acting, but he has a rock band. I said the magic words—*Jackson Sharpe*—and then to close the deal, I told him my father is looking for an unsigned group to do a cameo in his new movie. Suddenly he was all jazzed about playing Mike."

"Is that true?" Anna asked. "About your father looking for an unknown band?"

"Please." Sam waved a dismissive hand. "My father doesn't deal with those kinds of pissant details. I made it all up, but it's for a good cause. So I'll work with the actors this afternoon, and we'll shoot tonight with cue cards, compliments of Monty and a Magic Marker. It'll be a cinch to cut it in the editing room. Thank you for making our life easy."

Anna felt great. Who could have predicted that she'd turn out to be a writer? Her teachers had always told her that she had talent. She remembered a particularly excellent English teacher in middle school who had urged Anna to "let go more" with her writing. Well, maybe she was finally learning to do just that.

"Who's going to play Nina?" Anna asked.

"How about . . . you?" Sam suggested.

"Definitely not."

"It was worth a shot. I'd love to have Susan do it, then."

"Even less of a shot," Anna said. "She wouldn't even let them take her photo for Trinity's yearbook."

"Then it's going to be Dee," Sam warned. "Unless you change your mind about it being Cammie."

"No." Anna was emphatic. "Not Cammie. *Anyone* but Cammie."

"Speaking of, I have a confession to make. I mentioned to Cammie and Dee about Ben dumping you on New Year's Eve."

Anna barely blinked. In fact, she was so taken by Sam's honesty that she almost smiled. "Color me shocked."

"Okay, so you thought I would."

"Let's just say that the possibility crossed my mind."

"Fine. In that case, you can't get mad at me."

"Who's mad?" Anna asked. "I don't care what they know, and I care even less what they think."

"Cammie says she knows who the chick was."

"Sam, quit while you're ahead, okay?"

Sam reached for a crumpet that was on a dish on the table and took a thoughtful bite. "Like you don't want to know."

"I don't," Anna insisted.

"I'm not sure I believe you," Sam said. She put one hand atop Anna's script as if it were Anna's hand itself. "But you have excellent judgment."

She took a sip of her tea and made a face, then moved the cup to the far edge of their table. "Ugh. I'm never ordering this again. Look, I've always really liked Ben. But your sister is right. Ben's a player. You deserve better. Someone more tender, who will really under-stand you. And as smart as you, too."

"If you mean Adam, I told you before. I'm not interested in guys right now, Sam."

Sam rubbed a contemplative finger along the fili-greed iron table. "It's funny, because I'm starting to feel the same way. Sometimes I think all guys are buttholes. Once they get cloning right, men will be obsolete any-way. Ever wonder how much easier life would be if all of the coolest women just went gay?"

"Not really," Anna replied. This was a *very* strange conversation. "I don't think it's something you can choose."

Sam shrugged. "I'm not saying it's something that

can be faked, but it's a scientific fact that we're all inherently bisexual. Something to think about . . ."

Not likely. At the moment Anna had one or two more pressing things to think about than her own latent bisexuality. Time for a subject change.

"So . . . what's our next step?"

"Right. I'll ask the concierge to make more copies of your script. Then I'll make some shooting notes. I'll call at your suite when I'm done," Sam promised.

"Sounds like a plan," Anna said.

Dr. Fred

S am pushed the familiar number into her cell and paced while it rang. "Pick up, pick up, pick up," she murmured under her breath. The conversation she'd just had with Anna had been too weird. Because all through it she'd had to make a conscious effort to look at Anna's ear or chin. Because she had become so obsessed with Anna's mouth that it had taken all her concentration not to stare at it. She wasn't thinking about the movie she was about to shoot. She wasn't thinking about anything except Anna's lips.

Since it was a Saturday, she used Dr. Fred's home number. And while it was true she'd fired her psychotherapist a few days ago, she knew he'd be thrilled to take her back. Dr. Fred might be famous, with his own television show, but Sam's father had helped him get there by hiring him as her shrink. She'd been one of his first children-of-celebrity clients, and Jackson Sharpe had been one of the first guests on his show. The ratings had gone through the roof. Ergo, he owed her, big time.

"Hello?" Sam recognized his voice, with its distinctive flat midwestern vowels.

"Dr. Fred? It's Sam Sharpe."

"Sam! Good to hear from you!"

And so he comes crawling back, Sam thought. *No more "don't call me at home" or "wait until your next appointment." I knew it.*

"How are you, Sam?" Dr. Fred went on. "I've been concerned about you all year. Of course, the year's just a few days old." He laughed at his own unfunny joke.

Sam figured her best approach was to pretend that firing him had never happened. "I'm in Palm Springs with some friends. Things are weird."

"How so?"

"Well, there's this girl here. Her name is Anna. She's a new friend."

"Yes?"

"She's from New York. Smart. Gorgeous. Rich."

"Yes?"

"She's amazing. And talented. We're working on this student film for our English class? And she said she'd write the script for it. And I thought, 'Yeah, right. Go ahead. Write your script. But it's going to suck so much that I better write a secret backup script just in case.'"

"And?" Dr. Fred prompted.

"She can actually write. Her script was better than mine. Well, maybe."

"Did you tell her how good it was?"

Sam hesitated. She and Dr. Fred had been working through Sam's jealousy issue for a while. Dr. Fred would be very disappointed if he knew that Sam had told Anna her script was good, but "not great."

"Not really."

"Sam, just because Anna's good at something doesn't mean that you're not. There's no limit on how many people can be good at something."

"Okay, I'll work on that," Sam said dismissively. She had bigger fish to fry. "But that's not why I called. I called because I can't stop thinking about her."

"Can you be more specific, Sam?"

"Like . . . I want to kiss her," Sam confessed, her voice dropping low.

"Interesting."

"No, it isn't *interesting*," Sam snapped. "I told you, things are weird."

"Okay, so you would like to kiss this new friend," Dr. Fred responded. "How is that weird?"

"Let me run it by you again," Sam said slowly. "She's a *girl*."

"So, you're concerned that you're having sexual impulses toward this young lady?"

"It's not like I want to bone her," Sam insisted, her heart pounding. "I just want to kiss her. It's sort of like *Kissing Jessica Stein*, you know? Where the straight girl thinks she's attracted to a girl, but really she's straight and finally she ends up with this great guy in the end."

"Uh-hum," Dr. Fred murmured. "Except in that

movie the straight girl really is attracted to a gay girl. Is your new friend Anna gay?"

"No. Maybe. I don't know. She told me that she's taking a break from guys. That means she could be gay. Or at least bi."

"Or it could just mean that something happened in her life that makes her want to take a break from guys and concentrate on herself for a change. I think you feel threatened by this impulse," Dr. Fred surmised.

"No. Not really. Why would I be? It's not so unusual, is it? Or am I totally fucked up?"

"All of us have to remember that our self-worth is not determined by our sexuality," Dr. Fred declared. "Have you been repeating your affirmations?"

Dr. Fred and his fucking affirmations. He even had a new greeting card line out with those damn affirmations on them. *I create my own reality. I am a perfect being of light. I choose to be happy in the now.*

"No. They're stupid."

"How about if you reserve judgment on that. This all may have to do with your father, Sam. And your hostility toward Poppy. For now, say your affirmations and practice those breathing exercises I gave you. Don't be so hard on yourself."

"Yeah, yeah, yeah," Sam grumbled.

"I can make an opening for you at your old time on Wednesday," Dr. Fred went on. "Shall I expect you?"

"Yeah," Sam said grudgingly. At least Dr. Fred listened to her.

"Excellent. And Sam? Feeling something and acting on it are two different things. Remember that."

Sam hung up and sprawled out on the Swedish birch bed, directly under the tasteful nude oil painting of Marilyn Monroe. She didn't feel any less anxious. "Feeling something and acting on it are two different things," she mumbled aloud. But somehow it didn't make her feel any better.

Hello?

"According to Cammie, V's Saturday sunset cocktail parties are infamous," Susan told Anna. They were in Anna's suite, where Anna was dressing for the party. Susan was already dressed: she'd traded in her Lower East Side black for a very fitted red Patricia Field silk knit turtleneck with Chanel paisley velvet pants and strappy Miu Miu red high heels. In fact, the outfit looked like something Cammie would wear.

"Infamous for what?" Anna asked as she went into the bathroom to brush her hair.

"Evidently there aren't enough hetero guys to go around, so the party is the biggest catfight west of the Mississippi."

"Cammie is full of it. Women do not come to spas to get laid," Anna called to her sister through the half-open door. "Maybe too much shopping fried her brain."

Anna knew that Susan and Cammie had spent the afternoon at an off-price discount mall near the freeway. They'd passed it coming to town: it was the size of a small theme park and carried every label from Armani to Zou Zou.

"How would you know about spa cocktail parties? Whenever we went to a spa with Mom, your head was buried in a book." Susan pushed open the bathroom door and stuck her head inside. "Aren't you going to wear any makeup?"

"I don't like makeup."

"Jane Percy Junior," Susan teased. "So what's the scoop on Parker Pinelli? I met him this afternoon."

"Cute, nice, self-involved, not the brightest," Anna said. "If you change your mind and do the part of Nina in our film, you can find out for yourself."

Susan stretched. "I can find out anyway. And I don't care what his IQ is. I'm not interested in his mind."

"He's still in high school, Sooz. If you don't do Nina, it's going to be Dee."

"I don't even like to have my picture taken, Anna. You know that."

True. "Fine. Dee it is, then. Can you bring me my phone?" Anna remembered that she had to check in with Brock Franklin about the Steinbergs' party and see what time he wanted to be picked up. "And Brock's number at the hotel—they're in my purse."

"Brock is such an asshole. You remember my friend Alexandra Moir?" Susan called, then padded in with Anna's phone and Brock's number. "The one who dated him?"

"I thought *you* dated him."

"Once. But she was with him for like two months. Remember her?"

"She had red hair and really cute freckles, right?" Anna said.

"Yeah. Her dad owns half of Lower Manhattan. Your new friend Brock cheated on her with a girl from Wesleyan who got a story into that literary magazine *Granta.*"

"I'm not dating him. It's for work." Anna sat on the edge of the tub and placed the call—he'd already checked in but wasn't in his room. So she left a voice mail reminding Brock that she was Susan Percy's sister and would meet him at the hotel the next afternoon, at four, before the Steinbergs' party.

"Which Steinbergs?" Susan asked. "The old ones or the young ones?"

"I think the young ones. I know I'm supposed to know who they are, but I don't."

"They're only like the most powerful early-twenties couple in Hollywood. He directs, she writes and produces. The old Steinbergs do movies like—oh, forget it. You don't even care."

"Honestly? Not much."

"Don't be such a snob, Anna. There are movies without subtitles that are really good. We'll go to some when we get back to L.A. Why didn't you tell me in the first place that it was their party? I'd love to go!"

"See how well that worked out?" Anna asked brightly. She reached for a leather cord to tie her hair back.

"Still going for understated, I see," Susan noted.

Anna shrugged. "I'm comfortable with it."

"Comfort is highly overrated." Susan stretched, baring

her midriff. "God, what's a cocktail party without alcohol?"

"If you don't think you can handle it, stay here. Why tempt yourself?"

"Hide in my suite?" Susan scoffed. "Without temptation, life is boring."

As Susan went to the full-length mirror to check herself out, Anna scrutinized her in a different way. What had happened to her? Was this the Susan Percy who could speak four languages fluently, who always wore expensive and understated outfits in the best of taste? Or was it the Susan who majored in modern European history and wanted to end world hunger? And what about the Susan who lived in the squalid building on Avenue D, with the junkies lolling on her stoop?

"It was Bowdoin," Anna said flatly.

"What was?"

"When you started to drink."

Susan fluffed her hair. "Oh. That. Old news."

"Did something happen to you there, Sooz?"

"I got away from home, that's all. And decided to live the way I wanted to live. Why do you have to make everything into some kind of psychodrama?" There was an edge to her voice.

"It's just that you changed," Anna explained. "And I don't know why."

"Maybe what you should be asking is why you haven't," Susan said.

"What is that supposed to mean?"

Susan folded her arms. "You told me you came to California to change your life. Only you haven't changed at all."

Anna was taken aback. It was as if her sister was going on the attack. "It's only been a few days, Sooz."

"Yeah, but look who you're dating. Adam the nice guy."

"*Nice* isn't a dirty word, Susan. And besides, I broke up with him."

Susan looked surprised. "Since when?"

"Since you pointed out the error of my choose-some-one-safe ways," Anna replied. "It felt more like *use* some-one safe. I like Adam too much to lead him on like that."

"Well, aren't you the Girl Scout. So are you going back to the bad boy?"

"I just want to be alone for a while."

Susan laughed. "No girl wants to be alone."

Anna's temper flared. "It's not always about a guy, okay? No one forced you to hook up with that loser you were with in college."

Susan's face closed down. "You never met him. And don't make this about me, Anna."

"Fine, we'll make it about me, then."

"I can tell you exactly what's going to happen. You're going to spend about a month on this 'I am woman' thing, and Adam is just going to hang around anyway, waiting for you to change your mind. You'll like that—because you'll have even more power."

"God, you piss me off, Susan! That's not why I did it!"

"Lie to yourself if you want," Susan said blithely,

"but not to me. With him you run the show. Anna calls, Adam comes. Literally and figuratively."

"That's low," Anna said.

"And true. But what happens when you *aren't* in charge? What happens then?"

I know exactly what happens, Anna thought. *Ben happens.*

By the time Anna and Susan joined the cocktail party, it was already in full swing. As a string quartet played Mozart, the privileged and beautiful people mingled. Parker and Dee were at a table with a gorgeous redhead; Anna could see a copy of her screenplay in front of them. She scanned the bar: the middle-aged woman who had glommed on to Parker earlier was nursing a tall drink, shooting visual daggers in Parker's direction. Nearby, Sam was deep in conversation with Jamie Cresswell, the guy she'd found to play Mike. Monty Pinelli was cradling a handheld, high-resolution video camera and was talking with one of the spa managers.

As Susan and Anna approached, Parker rose to greet them. He kissed Anna on the cheek, shook Susan's hand warmly, and then went to find two chairs. A moment later he was introducing them to the beautiful redhead, whose name was Prima McNaughton. She was visiting with her parents from Texas. Prima had an unusual tic. Whenever Parker faced in her direction, she'd lean in close enough so that her breasts would massage his arm.

Susan looked closely at the girl. "Wait, did you say your name was Prima McNaughton?"

"Uh-huh."

"Is your mother really slender?" Susan asked.

"Yeah. Why?"

Susan got a concerned look on her face. "Thank God I ran into you. I saw her just now by the valet stand at the main building. She's looking for you. I remember because your name is so unusual. She looked frantic."

"I swear, it's like I'm on a leash," Prima drawled with a sigh. She stood up. "I'll catch up with y'all."

Susan wagged her fingers at Prima as she walked off. "So, Parker, we meet again," she said seductively, and Anna realized that her sister had just pulled what Anna thought of as a Cammie. That is, she'd invented a story to rid the immediate world of Prima so that she could move in on Parker.

"Hey, Susan. You look great," Parker said. "Can we get you ladies a drink?"

"Anything nonalcoholic and fruity," Susan said easily.

"Same for me," Anna agreed.

Parker craned around and waved a discreet finger to get the waiter's attention, then touched the screenplay on the table. "The monologues you wrote are great, Anna," he said. "I had no idea you were a writer."

"Thanks," Anna said. "Honestly? Neither did I."

"I love my monologue, too," Dee said. "'I don't even know who I am,'" she recited in her girlish voice, practicing one of her lines. "Wow, that is so true. You could totally become a screenwriter, Anna. Are you going to be there when we film tomorrow morning?"

Anna had suggested to Sam that they should shoot the monologues off in the desert in the morning so as to take advantage of the early morning sun. She thought that the daylight close-ups would look striking against all the nighttime and indoor shooting they'd be doing. Sam had readily agreed and had even praised her on her visual sensitivity.

Anna nodded. "Yes, in case I need to make any last-minute changes. You never know. In fact, right after this party I'm going back to my suite. I'm not happy with one of the Mike monologues, and I want to do some rewrites. It's weird, like I can't get the lines out of my head."

"You don't need to do rewrites," Parker insisted. "Your first draft is better than most of the crap I have to read at auditions."

"Thanks," Anna said, surprised at the level of excitement over the project. Especially since Sam's response to it had been fairly tepid.

"So, when are you filming the rest of it?" Susan asked after the waiter had signaled he'd be right there.

"Sam and Monty are going to start shooting the background stuff here at the party any minute," Anna told her. "The last sequence will be in the Mount St. Helens sauna late tonight."

"Sounds hot and sweaty," Susan said, laughing. "And fun."

Parker raised his eyebrows and smiled mischievously. "It could be. But I heard you didn't want to be in the film."

Susan pursed her lips. "I might let you talk me into it."

Parker leaned closer to Susan. "What would it take to get you to change your mind?"

"Mmm. I'm not sure yet. But I'm willing to find out if you are."

Susan and Parker gazed into each other's eyes, and Anna decided that she couldn't take another moment of it. This party was a waste of time. Every moment that she sat there was another moment that she wasn't working on her screenplay. And Mike's opening monologue was bothering her more and more. Despite Sam's assurances that it was shootable, Anna didn't think it was exactly right.

"Excuse me," she said, rising. "I'm going to go back to work."

Dee said see you later, but all that Susan and Parker could manage was a halfhearted wave. Anna sent up a silent prayer that her sister was using birth control and then departed to her suite. A couple of hours with her screenplay, her laptop, and her printer seemed extremely inviting.

It was a few hours before Anna looked up from her laptop. She'd had no idea so much time had passed. Mike's monologue was much better now, more honest. She reread the last few lines.

"People can call it passion. Or lust. Or obsession. I don't really care. When I'm with her, touching her, is the only time I feel completely alive. If you've never felt the power of that, then I feel sorry for you."

Anna got up and stretched out the kink in her neck. Before Ben, she never could have written those lines because before Ben, she had never known those feelings. If she could have gone back in time and magically make it so they'd never met, she wouldn't have done it. Because along with the pain was the sweetness of feeling all that she'd felt for him. Part of her wanted him to know that. It didn't even matter about the girl on the promenade.

But how can I? He thinks I'm with Adam, Anna realized. *I want him to know that I didn't replace him with anyone except myself. That I don't just date people to keep from being lonely. Ben should know that I'm alone. By choice.*

Suddenly, correcting Ben's impression that she was with Adam became Anna's top priority. She got Ben's number from her PalmPilot. Then she took her cell phone from her purse, but the battery was dead—she'd forgotten to recharge it. Impulsively she reached for the hotel's phone on the desk and placed the call to Ben's cell.

"Hello?"

Ben's voice! Anna's first reaction was to hang up. No, that was ridiculous. She was being mature. She was in control. "Hi, Ben, it's Anna."

"Anna."

His voice was like a caress. Suddenly she felt ridiculous. Was she supposed to just blurt out that she and Adam weren't together? Now, too late, she realized that it would sound pathetically flirtatious. She'd broken up with Ben! Why would he care whether it was because she was with Adam, Mickey Mouse, or anyone at all?

Answer: he wouldn't.

"I'm sorry, I shouldn't have called," she began.

"Yes, you should!" he said quickly. "I was just think-ing about you."

Anna's hand was actually moist on the phone; that was how nervous she was. "I was going to tell you that Adam and I aren't seeing each other anymore. But now it sounds ridiculous."

"Not at all," he assured her. "Where are you?"

"It doesn't matter. I shouldn't have—"

"Would you stop it, Anna? Where the hell are you?"

"It's not what you think, Ben," Anna went on, feel-ing worse by the minute. "I don't want to be with any-one now."

Silence. "Wait. You called to tell me that *you want to be alone?*"

"I'm sorry, Ben, really."

"Anna, what the hell—?"

She hung up, her hands shaking. God, what an idiot she was! Why the hell *had* she called him? What per-verse part of her brain had decided that was a good idea?

Anna went into the bedroom and lay down on the bed. What an utterly fucked-up thing to do. She was disgusted with herself. Who the hell was *she* to judge Susan's behavior when her own was so pathetic?

For that, she had no answer at all.

Mount St. Helens

The Mount St. Helens sauna at V's spa had gotten its name for a good reason—the lava rocks in the sauna reputedly had been gathered only from the slopes of the active volcano in Washington. Allegedly the sauna had special healing powers. As Anna hurried down the marble staircase to the lower-level saunas in the main spa building, she hoped the sauna lived up to it's reputation, because Sam was going to tear her limb from limb—she was already forty-five minutes late. That she'd been in her suite working on her screenplay and oblivious to the time was a pretty lame excuse. After her aborted phone call with Ben she'd gone back to work and lost track of the time.

Once on the bottom level, she read the plates on each wooden door. Seaweed Hydro Sauna. Serenity Purification Sauna. Ah, there it was: Mount St. Helens Sauna.

Anna hung her white terry-cloth robe on a hook outside the sauna and went in. She was relieved to see that everyone in the enormous cedar-planked room sported a bathing suit. Parker had on surfer jams. At his feet was the middle-aged woman who'd been pursuing him all day. Cammie was stretched out on the highest bench in a spectacular white Gottex one-piece with very revealing cutouts. Dee and Jamie Cresswell sat together on the top tier across from Cammie— there was a slew of other guests, too. Meanwhile Sam and Monty were manning two different cameras—film was rolling.

"Nice of you to join us, Anna," Sam said.

"Sorry I'm late. I was writing."

Sam waved it off. "We're fine."

"What can I do to help?"

"Nada. It's under control. Just sit."

Grateful that Sam hadn't embarrassed her further, Anna found a place along the far wall. Parker came over to her and gave her a big hug. Anna was caught off guard. Yes, she knew Parker, but it wasn't like they were close friends. "Hey, come join me," he said.

Then Monty aimed his camera at them and Anna realized that this was all for the purpose of the film.

"We were just talking about the Steinbergs' party on Sunday," Parker said. "Your sister said you'd be there."

"Um, yes," Anna said. She felt self-conscious and inhibited. She'd *told* Sam she didn't want to be in this film. Was this some form of passive-aggressive payback?

"With Brock 'I'm-So-Pretentious' Franklin," Susan added.

"Yeah, yeah, we're up to speed," Cammie said. "Anna

is an intern at my dad's new agency. That could be interesting."

"I'm not working for him," Anna said.

"Actually, Anna, if you work at Apex, you are," Cammie shot back.

"You know, Cammie, maybe your dad would like to talk about taking me on as a client," Parker said. "I'm up for a new drama on the WB. About rich kids in Beverly Hills."

"How *90210* is that?" Cammie asked, rolling over onto her back. A small, hairy guy in his fifties smiled lasciviously, enjoying the scenery.

Anna was confused. "Our zip code?"

The hairy guy laughed. "She's shining you on. It was a TV show, back in the day. I had an overall deal at Fox at the time."

"Excuse me, Stevie, Stewie—what did you say your name was?" Cammie interrupted.

"Stanley."

"Stanley," Cammie repeated. "We don't care."

Dee, who'd been lying down behind Parker, sat up. "You seriously don't know what *90210* was, Anna?"

Anna shook her head.

"It was all about rich kids in Beverly Hills," Dee explained.

"Like ten years ago, Dee," Cammie said.

"Well, yeah, but there are reruns on cable all the time." Dee turned toward Sam, who craned her camera up to focus on her. "You know, Sam, some people say that you remind them of Tori Spelling." Dee ticked off the reasons on her fingers. "Her father is a famous producer. She wanted to be in the business, so he got her a role on *Beverly Hills 90210*, which he produced. And I read how she was always kind of insecure about her looks—"

"Cut!" Sam yelled, tilting her camera down and glaring at Monty until he turned his off, too. "Dee, this is not supposed to be about *me*. We're making a *film*."

"Well, yeah, but it's supposed to be real, isn't it?" Dee asked. "Besides, you told us before Anna arrived that Parker should try to get with Anna. So I'm just trying to up the dramatic tension."

"Always good to know you're listening, Dee," Sam said drily. "How about some steam in here? Okay, let's roll again."

Monty started filming as Parker poured cold water on the glowing lava rocks. A few wisps of white steam rose toward the ceiling.

"More," Cammie commanded, obviously too comfortable to move.

"If we do that, we won't be able to see you," Monty said.

"No, wait, let's try it," Sam decided. "Because right now you people are giving me nothing. Maybe more steam will loosen you up. Use the valve."

Sam pointed to a steam intake valve on the floor; Parker obliged by opening the valve all the way. A geyser of steam shot into the sauna, enough to obscure everyone from view.

"Perfect," Sam chortled. "Parker, turn it off. As soon as we can make out faces, Monty, start the film again."

Then Anna heard the door open. Someone entered, but she couldn't see who it was because of the thick steam. She recognized the voice, though. She'd recognize it anywhere.

"Anna, are you in here?" the voice called. "It's Ben."

Payback

No one screwed with Prima McNaughton and got away with it.

Sure, Prima was furious with herself for falling for that lame story about her mother looking for her. But it was that Susan Percy chick who would have to pay. Prima knew that Parker and Susan were going to be in one of the spa saunas later as part of some student film. That was all she needed.

Bikini in hand, Prima hurried down the stairs of the spa services building, nearly colliding at the bottom of the stairwell with an incredibly hot guy. Tall and buff, with short brown hair and blue eyes, he wore a shirt the color of his eyes and perfectly fitting jeans.

Whoa. Time out. Susan could wait. Thank goodness Prima had on her Miu Miu minidress and Manolo Blahnik sky-high sandals—this boy made Parker look like a geek. Time to go into flirt mode.

Prima introduced herself. The guy said his name was Ben; he was looking for a friend. Someone at the front desk had told him that Sam Sharpe was filming in the Mount St. Helens sauna; did she know where that one was?

Prima had done her homework and pointed confidently to the third door on the left. Was Ben going to change? Because Prima was just about to put on her bikini—she waved the pink material coquettishly. Maybe they could sauna together?

But this Ben dude had a one-track mind. He was looking for Sam and another girl named Anna Percy. He had to find them.

Anna Percy? Was it that bitch Susan Percy's sister? It was a damn conspiracy!

Ben left Prima and went into the sauna as Prima watched, hands on hips. It was payback time. Someone had left a long metal exercise pole in the corner. Perfect. When the sauna door had closed completely, Prima propped the pole against the door handle and wedged the other end against the far wall.

Bingo. They were locked in.

Oh, she knew there was probably an emergency button in there. V's had to cover their ass in case some old codger had a heart attack midsteam and needed help. But it would probably take a while for anyone to find it and use it and even longer for someone to get to the sauna from the main building.

Prima smiled. Revenge really was sweet. She tossed her glossy red curls over her shoulder. Then she walked away as quickly as her high-priced shoes could carry her.

Red Button

Anna felt as if she couldn't breathe, but it had nothing to do with sauna heat. Insane, bizarre, but true—Ben Birnbaum, fully clothed, was just a few feet from her. The questions were, how? And why?

"Ben?" she asked, completely taken aback.

"So this is Ben Birnbaum, the bad boy," Susan piped up. "Interesting entrance. I'm Anna's sister, Susan."

"Anna, can I talk to you? Please?" Ben asked.

"What, and leave us out of this sweet moment?" Cammie asked, her tone cutting. "I hope you're recording this for posterity, Sam."

"The camera is off," Sam said.

Anna felt Sam staring at her as she turned back to Ben. "How'd you even know I was here? I never said where I was!"

"I have caller ID. Look, I'm melting through my clothes. Please. I just need five minutes."

Anna had forgotten that she'd called Ben from the hotel phone. Not the best move. But now he was here, so she'd have to deal with him. *In private.*

She nodded stiffly and slid off the wooden slats. Ben turned and pushed the sauna door. It didn't budge.

He pushed again. Nothing.

"I think it's stuck," he said, putting some real muscle in a third try. "Great, this is the topper to everything."

"Just push the frigging red button next to the door," the hairy guy said, disgusted. "Someone will come from the main building."

"In the meantime," Cammie chimed in, "we'd all love to know what Ben is so desperate to tell Anna."

"*Anna*, Cammie," Ben said firmly. "Not you."

He had already perspired through his T-shirt, so he pulled it over his head.

"Should I provide appropriate striptease music?" Susan asked sweetly.

Anna groaned. Her sister was adding fuel to the proverbial fire, though Anna had to admit that Ben's taut torso was sweaty perfection. "Maybe I can shine some light on this, Ben," Susan went on. "Anna thinks the only reason you want her back is because she doesn't want you anymore."

Ben looked at Anna. "Did you tell her that?"

Anna stared at the sauna door, willing it to open. "I really do not want to talk about this right here."

"It's because Anna and Adam are a couple now," Dee told Ben.

"She broke up with Adam," Susan put in.

"Shut *up!*" Dee cried. "When did this happen?"

"Can everyone please—?" Anna began.

No one was listening to her. "It's not like Anna confides in you, Dee," Cammie put in.

"So, Ben," Susan began, "do you know that Dee's been telling everyone she did you up at Princeton?"

"Susan!" Anna protested.

"Come on, Anna. What does all the let's-keep-everything-private bullshit get you? You think Mom is happy? You think any of her friends are happy?"

"Jeez," Ben muttered. "I'm in a psychodrama."

"Then you must be the psycho—you're the one standing in a sauna half dressed, my dear," said the middle-aged woman near Parker. "When's security going to get here? I'm completely dehydrated."

Cammie turned on Dee. "Is that true? Did you sleep with Ben?"

"So what if it is?" Dee challenged. "It was when I was on my college tour. You guys weren't even together anymore."

"We didn't have sex, Dee," Ben insisted.

"Yes, we did. You got toasted, so you just don't remember, maybe," Dee declared. "But I remember. Every single moment."

"Tell him the rest," Susan urged.

"It's a secret," Dee said.

Susan shook her head. "Don't you think you owe Ben the truth?"

That was when Anna realized "the truth" to which Susan was referring. Dee must have told Susan the same thing that she'd told Anna—that she was pregnant with Ben's baby.

Dee hesitated. "It's a little premature."

"Look, sweetheart. It's either true or it isn't true," Susan said. "Either you're pregnant or you're not."

"*What?*" Ben bellowed.

Dee bit her lower lip. "Well, I haven't been to a doctor yet, exactly."

Ben threw his hands in the air. "This is insane!"

"Buddy, is there anyone in here besides me you haven't screwed?" the hairy guy asked.

Ben ignored him. "You're not pregnant, Dee."

"How do you know?" Dee countered. "I might be."

Sam cleared her throat loudly, getting everyone's attention. "Really. Then why did you knock on my door last night and ask if I had any tampons?"

"Bus-ted!" Susan chortled.

The only sound in the sauna was the faint hiss of heat rising from the lava rocks.

"Well, I thought I was," Dee began, her voice meek. "I mean, maybe I was, for a little while." She buried her face in her hands. "You are all being so rude."

Anna stood. "This is horrible," she declared. "Whatever happened between Dee and Ben is between them. And whatever happened between Ben and me is between us. I don't care what any of you think." Her eyes swept from Sam, to Dee, to Cammie. "And you three. You claim to be each other's best friends. But you take such . . . such glee in each other's miseries. What is *wrong* with you people?"

The sauna was silent. Even Cammie had the grace to look somewhat guilty, at least momentarily.

Finally the older woman broke the silence. "Take it from me, girls. Never go for a pretty boy. Marry a man who is a lot older, uglier, and richer than you are. If you're good enough in bed, he won't even demand a prenup."

With those pearls of wisdom the door flew open and two burly security guards stepped into the sauna in front of a *whoosh* of cool air. "Are you people all right?" one of them asked.

"More than all right," Monty crowed as he turned off *his* video camera. "I got that whole friggin' thing on tape!"

Why Turn a Comedy Into a Tragedy?

"Anna! Dammit, Anna!" Ben called.

Anna charged out the door of the spa services building, determined not to look back. But then Ben was next to her.

"Where are you going?"

She stared straight ahead. "Someplace that isn't here."

"Hey, you're the one who called me, remember?"

"Chalk it up to temporary insanity," Anna decided.

He kept pace as she strode through the lush gardens that led to the main building. "Look, I wasn't expecting a showdown in the sauna, Anna. I didn't plan that."

"Fine. You didn't plan it."

"So why are you blaming me, then?"

She whirled on him so quickly, he took an involuntary step backward. "Blame? Blame has nothing to do with anything. Do you see the kind of people you call friends, Ben? Sam is supposed to be your friend, but even she calls you a player. Dee? She's pathetic. And Cammie is a coldhearted bitch."

"Don't judge me by them—"

"Fine, I'll judge you by what I know of you. You say you don't know whether or not you had sex with Dee because you were too wasted to remember. What kind of a person does that, Ben? You say you had to dump me on New Year's because you went to rescue a friend. Then you don't even contact me for three days to offer that lame excuse! Or were you drunk that time, too? You don't get to abdicate responsibility for your behavior because you got up close and personal with Johnny Walker Red!"

"It's not something I . . . The situation was . . ." Ben stopped. He sighed. His shoulders drooped. "Okay. Maybe you're right."

He looked so sad that Anna momentarily wanted to put her arms around him. "You're lucky that Dee isn't pregnant, Ben," Anna said, her voice softer now. "But don't you see? You don't remember what happened that night, which means it could have been true. *Then* what would you have done?"

"I don't know." His voice was ragged, his eyes miserable. "For what it's worth, I'm sorry, Anna. I wish I could explain so you'd understand . . . but I guess it doesn't matter to you anymore. I'm sorry I bothered you."

He shoved his hands in his pockets and walked away. Anna couldn't help it; she felt as if Ben had lifted her heart out of her chest and was taking it with him. Or, more accurately, dragging it behind him. She had to force herself not to follow him.

It was over. Really over. There was nothing left to say.

*   *   *

When Anna got back to the suite building, her sister stood outside her door.

"Well, that was entertaining," Susan said as Anna let them inside.

"So happy to provide your post-rehab amusement."

"Wow. I don't think I've ever heard sarcasm from you before," Susan commented.

Anna flopped onto the couch, lay down, and closed her eyes. "How can you find this funny?"

"Because it is. Why turn a comedy into a tragedy?"

Anna opened her eyes again. Susan was at the desk, scanning the room service menu. "What if I had said that to you?"

"Bravo, score one for the kid sister. Want a snack?"

"Guess what, Susan? It's possible to have real problems in this life without having to go to rehab over them."

Susan kept her eyes on the menu. "I know that," she said quietly.

Tears filled Anna's eyes as she sat up. "What happened to you, Sooz?"

Susan looked up from the menu. "What are you talking about?"

"The person in this room with me . . . this isn't you."

"Maybe it is."

"No. You were never cold. Or mean. Or bitchy. You were always . . . you cared about people. You cared about me."

Susan put down the menu and walked over to one of

the plush chairs. She sat on it with one of her legs slung over an armrest. "Maybe I just don't want to feel so much anymore, Anna. Life is easier that way."

"That's too simple," Anna said. She hadn't planned on confronting Susan, especially after what had happened in the sauna. She hadn't even consciously realized how much Susan's behavior had been bothering her. But here they were.

"Why, because I decided not to play by Mom's rules anymore?" Susan asked. "All the caveats and addendums of what is and isn't permissible? God forbid you have appetites. God forbid you have passion. Mom's rules suck, Anna. I'd rather live my way and fuck it up than be stuck in that prison. I said this to you before, and I'll say it again now: When is the last time you took a chance on anything?"

"Coming to Los Angeles was a big chance, and we're not talking about me."

"Right," Susan shot back. "Because you'd much rather focus on my problems than on yours. So you moved to Los Angeles. Big deal. Nothing changed except the ocean."

Anna felt her hands clench into fists. "Fine. I'll try it your way. How does it go again? Drop out of school to live with some lowlife loser. Get all fucked up. Then go to rehab and bail on it. Then become loser party babe. Have I got that right?"

All the color drained from Susan's face. "I didn't bail on rehab."

"Yes, you did," Anna insisted. "At least own up to your—"

"I got kicked out," Susan snapped. "Happy?"

Anna was silent. She had no idea what to say. Until finally she came up with, "Of course I'm not happy. What happened?"

Susan stared at the carpet, as if she couldn't bear to face her sister. "I didn't get high, if that's what you think." Finally she raised her eyes. "I was with a guy. He was getting high. We got caught. And I'm not going to ask you if you believe me because I don't give a damn. So fuck you, Anna, and the sanctimonious horse you rode in on." Susan got up and stormed out the door.

Anna sat there, stunned. She knew Susan was in pain. There had to be secrets Susan hadn't shared. But instead of being there for her sister, she'd attacked her. The worst part of it was, Anna knew how upset it had made Susan when her father had done the exact same thing.

Size Six

"Forty-eight, forty-nine, fifty!"

Cammie sat up on the incline stomach-crunch bench, having just finished her fifth set of crunches.

"Impressive," Susan said, wiping her neck with a towel. She'd just finished doing three miles on an elliptical machine.

It was the next day. Cammie had called Susan at the Beverly Hills Hotel and invited her to come work out with her at the Summit, the most exclusive fitness club in Los Angeles. Occupying the penthouse and roof of the tallest building in Century City, the Summit attracted actors, models, studio executives, and celebrities who were not at all put off by the five-figure annual membership fee and who would not be caught dead in, say, L.A. Fitness, regardless of whether Cindy Crawford did their advertisements or not.

The Summit was massive. The Summit was plush. There was a rooftop swimming pool, four lighted tennis courts, an indoor basketball court, a climbing wall, a restaurant and juice bar, aerobics, yoga, spinning, and kick-boxing studios, plus all the weight-lifting, circuit training, and cardio equipment that anyone could want. What members liked the most—aside from being insulated from the Los Angeles riffraff, and the incredible vistas through the glass walls from the Pacific to downtown—was that once they were out on the fitness floor, there was none of the pretense that ruined so many other clubs. Even if the clients *were* on the covers of major magazines, everyone dressed down to work out. Which was why both Cammie and Susan were wearing ordinary gym shorts and T-shirts with athletic shoes. This was perhaps the only "in" spot in Los Angeles where it was "out" to preen, except in the sense that everyone checked out the perfection—or lack thereof—of everyone else's shape.

"Ready to pack it in?" Cammie asked, wiping the damp hair off her forehead.

Susan agreed. Cammie led the way to the locker room, which featured floor-to-ceiling glass walls—the glass was one-way so no helicopter-borne paparazzi with a supertelephoto lens could snap any embarrassing photographs. "Did you call Anna and tell her that you're bringing me to the Steinbergs' party?"

Susan opened her locker. "No."

"Why not?"

"We had a fight last night. Coming back from the desert, we barely said a word to each other."

Perfect. Cammie had studied Susan and Anna's relationship. Susan was Anna's weak link. And, by extension, her sacrificial lamb.

Cammie cursed herself for not having been able to hold on to Ben Birnbaum. And she cursed Anna Percy for having such power over him. Ben had come for Anna, right into the Mount St. Helens sauna, fully dressed. He'd never done anything like that for her, and he never would. It hurt so much to know that he loved Anna in a way he'd never loved her.

For that, Anna would pay.

As Cammie stripped down, she was careful to keep the smirk off her face. Susan was emotionally dependent on Anna; that, Cammie had already figured out. A fight between them was definitely something she could use to her advantage. Poor little Susan could so easily come unmoored without Anna to prop her up.

Cammie stretched, knowing that her naked body was fabulous. In contrast to Susan's, whose stomach was fleshy and whose ass sagged a little. After they'd undressed for the shower, Susan wrapped a towel around herself and tucked in the end.

"So, what was the big fight about?" Cammie asked.

"I'd rather not talk about it."

Cammie laughed. "You sound just like your sister."

"Who sounds just like our mother. Who probably writes a thank-you note after sex." The edge of Susan's towel came untucked, revealing her naked body. "God, I wish I'd lose the weight from rehab already."

Cammie's eyes flicked over Susan's body before Susan retucked the towel. "Doesn't it suck? The same thing happened to me when I was in rehab."

"I've already dropped three pounds," Susan said. "Two more weeks, I'll take off the rest."

"Well, I admire your self-confidence. I mean, it must suck, having such a perfect sister."

Susan just shrugged.

They spent the next half hour in the marble-and-glass shower and the steam room. Cammie made sure that she let her eyes stray over the small fleshy roll at Susan's waist, then when Susan "caught" her, she pretended she hadn't been staring. She pointed out the gorgeous hard bodies of the other women they saw. And made a joke that it was illegal to be over a size six at the Summit.

"So, what are you going to wear to the party?" Cammie asked as they headed back to the locker room area.

"The black pants we got at Betsey Johnson."

"Those? Oh. Great." Cammie made sure doubt colored her declaration.

Susan dropped her towel into the wet-towel bin and took her clothes from her locker. "What? You helped me pick them out!"

"They're great," Cammie assured her. "You and Anna have such different styles."

"So?" Susan hooked her bra and reached for her T-shirt.

"Just that Anna would never wear the pants you bought."

Susan pulled on her panties, then her jeans. "I could wear something else."

"No, it's cool. You have your own taste. I mean, you like that look. It's fine."

"What look?"

"You know, that I'm-so-fucking-cool look. You're rebelling, it's fine."

"Thank you, Dr. Fred," Susan muttered.

"I know just how you feel," Cammie went on. Susan was sitting on the bench, strapping on her sandals, so Cammie sat next to her, leaning close, her voice low and hypnotic.

"Do you ever feel like if you let yourself give in to everything you want, that you'd just never stop wanting?"

"All the time," Susan confessed. She reached for the other sandal.

"Like you'll never measure up. And nothing can fill you up, ever," Cammie went on, "because you're just this gluttonous, needy *thing?* I feel that way all the time."

Susan looked around. The locker room was empty. No one was there to overhear their conversation. "Well, don't you hide it well."

"Do I?" Cammie feigned surprise. She pulled her Giuseppe Zanotti suede-and-leather sandals out of her locker. "Thanks. I'm telling you, Susan, after rehab, I was afraid to do anything. Eating was out—I was such a pig. Drinking—how was I supposed to stop at one drink? Pot—I'd want to smoke my way into oblivion and stay there. Coke, E, sex—anything I ever did before rehab, I wanted to do and do and do."

"So, how'd you stop?"

Cammie pulled on her silk lace Miu Miu T-shirt. "I had to prove that I could master it, you know? I mean, what was I supposed to do, stay alone in my room listening to Ani DiFranco for the rest of my life? So I just, you know, had one drink."

Cammie could see the yearning for "one drink" on Susan's face.

"And?" Susan prompted.

"And so what? Seriously, that's the conclusion I came to. If I have one or two drinks, so what? It made me feel better. It didn't hurt anyone. And I proved I could party and not, like, just pass out."

"Must be nice." Susan stood up, zipped her jeans, and pulled on her Chanel shirt.

"It *is* nice." Cammie reached deep into her gym bag, rooted around, and found what she was looking for: a pint of Flagman vodka, its Russian label proving that it was authentic. She unscrewed the cap. "I can't stand for people to tell me what to do. You want some?"

"No." Susan sprayed her neck with Escada perfume, then started to brush her hair and put on lip gloss.

"Fine. I understand. Personally, I'd like to say a big 'fuck you' to Anna and everyone else who thinks they know exactly how I should be and who I should be." Cammie took a long, dramatic swallow. She could feel Susan's eyes on her. "Oh yeah. Nothing else feels like that. Sure you don't want some?"

"No."

"You're right. If you're really out of control, I mean. One sip and you'll be lap dancing for Jell-O shots." Cammie upended the bottle again.

"I'm not out of control."

"Anna thinks you are. Otherwise why would she be playing *Baby Sitters Club* with you?" Cammie tilted the bottle to her lips one more time; she could feel Susan's yearning as the fiery liquid rolled down her gullet. "Mmm. Nothing takes the edge off like Flagman, you know? Makes Stoli taste like Drano."

Susan didn't answer, but Cammie could see she was gritting her teeth as she worked the hairbrush.

"But listen," Cammie went on. "I completely understand. I guess Anna is right. You're this out-of-control loser who can never have a drink again. It sounds like a death sentence, but you know what's best for you."

"When did I say I was never going to drink again?"

Cammie shrugged. "I was where you are once. For me, the only way to conquer the fear was to do what scared me and prove I could handle it. But I guess you're different."

Susan glared at her. "That's bullshit."

"Prove it, then. Loser." Cammie held the vodka out to Susan.

For a long moment Susan stared at the bottle like it was Pandora's box. Cammie could sense her wavering.

"Why should I?" Susan asked, her eyes on the open bottle.

"To prove it doesn't have power over you. To prove you're not the fat loser your sister thinks you are."

Another long beat, then Susan grabbed the bottle

from Cammie's hands. "My sister is right about you, you know. You really are a bitch."

Their eyes held. For a moment Cammie thought Susan was going to dump the vodka onto the floor of the locker room. But instead Susan lifted the bottle to her mouth and took a long swallow.

Bingo.

Home Theater

The Steinbergs' own huge home in the Hollywood Hills was in the midst of a complete renovation, so their party was being held at the Graystone mansion on Loma Vista Drive in Beverly Hills. As Anna drove Brock from his hotel to the party, he was utterly silent, except to mention to Anna that he'd recently taken up Buddhism and always felt out of sorts when he visited Los Angeles. "I guess I'm destined to live and die in New York City," he said.

She smiled and stopped at a light on Santa Monica Boulevard. He didn't look very different from how Anna remembered him in New York: short and skinny, with straight dark hair that fell boyishly over one eye, he wore black jeans and a black T-shirt under an oversized black sports jacket and the latest variation of Pumas on his feet. He was quieter, though. And far nicer than she'd remembered.

Anna had chosen her clothes carefully—a simple raw-silk black Chanel sleeveless dress that had belonged to her mother. Her only accessory was a white-gold chain around her neck that had been a sixteenth-birthday gift from Susan. She'd left her hair loose; it fell in a glossy, straight line to her shoulders.

Brock peered out the window. "Think these mansions are close enough together? You could be in the crapper, run out of toilet paper, and call to the next house for a roll."

"Land is very expensive here," Anna said as the light turned green.

"These people just want to prove they have the biggest-ass house," Brock told her. "It's all so meaningless."

"I guess," Anna said diplomatically, discreet enough not to remind him that he'd just dropped three-quarters of a million dollars on an apartment in Chelsea that wasn't even fifteen hundred square feet.

A few minutes later she pulled her Lexus up in front of the impressive stone mansion. A valet opened her door and helped her out; another opened Brock's door for him. Brock put his hands together in a prayerful gesture and did a slight bow to thank him. The door to the mansion was open, and they could hear the party in full swing.

"Ready?" Anna asked.

When Brock nodded, they stepped inside and wended their way through the beautiful people to the massive living room. Its cathedral ceiling made the room seem even larger than it was; the furnishings ranged from dark and Gothic to eclectic contemporary. There were teal, hand-carved, trilevel Chinese end tables adorned with carvings of dragons; sofas of deep, lush velvet; and purple tapestry throw pillows. A magnificent saltwater aquarium had been built directly onto an oversized coffee table. In various nooks around the room green and red velvet paisley cushions created conversation areas. There was even a wood fire roaring in the stone fireplace.

Anna looked around for her sister. After the silent drive back to Los Angeles with Sam, they'd dropped Susan at her bungalow. Anna had tried to call her in the early afternoon to make peace, but there was no answer. All she'd been able to do was leave the address of the party on Susan's voice mail, make a brief apology for her part in their fight, and say that she hoped to see her sister later.

However, Susan was nowhere to be found. But there were plenty of movie-industry people. She even had a couple of celebrity sightings—the ebullient Italian actor-director Roberto Benigni. She recognized him from his Oscar-winning film, *Life Is Beautiful.* The French actor Gerard Depardieu. He'd been in the movie *Roxanne*, a takeoff on *Cyrano de Bergerac.*

"Brock!" A small, balding man in a red baseball jacket pushed through the crowd and joined them. "Kenny Kendall—we spoke on the phone last week. Margaret Cunningham at Apex put us together. I directed *Case Sensitive.* She sent you the DVD. It's going to be at Sundance this year."

"Right, right," Brock said, shaking his hand. "Brilliant work, man."

"Speaking of, I caught *Uptown/Downtown* in New

York last week." His hands fluttered toward his face. "Hot, hot, hot. *Adored* it."

"Hey, I just try to put the truth out there," Brock said.

"That's why your work spoke to me." He squeezed Brock's nonexistent biceps and moved closer. Since Brock hadn't bothered to introduce Anna, she figured this was her cue.

"Hello, I'm Anna Percy, with Apex." She held out her hand.

Kenny gave her a dead-carp handshake, his eyes glued to Brock. "Listen, we absolutely have to work together. The German financing for my new film should come through next week. *Double Samurai.* It's the spiritual quest of a man in pain searching for something to believe in. Harrison is attached to star, but frankly, it needs a top-to-bottom rewrite. I'll call Margaret. Listen, you want to meet Harrison?"

"Sure," Brock said. "I'd love to."

"Cool. Come on!"

Before Anna could open her mouth, Kenny had put his hand on Brock's elbow and was steering him through the crowd. What was she supposed to do, trot after him? No, that would be ludicrous. Why hadn't Margaret sent a real agent to this party, someone who would know what to do?

"Hello, Anna."

Anna turned around. Dee Young stood before her. "What are you doing here?"

"My dad did the music for Krissy Steinberg's last

movie, so we got to be friends. I just want you to know, Anna, I've decided to turn over a new leaf."

"Mm-hm," Anna mumbled, since she had little comprehension of what Dee was talking about and even less interest.

"My life coach told me that I have the power to reinvent myself."

"What's a life coach?"

"She helps me plan my path." Dee's hands went to her flat stomach. "She helped me realize that while I was *psychologically* pregnant with Ben's baby, it wasn't a physical reality."

Without a doubt, Dee needed someone a bit better trained psychologically than a "life coach." But now wasn't the time for Anna to offer her counsel. She had to find Brock. "Excuse me, I need to use . . ." Anna pointed toward the powder room.

"All right." Dee gave Anna a quick hug and waved as Anna walked away. As soon as Dee was out of sight, Anna scurried toward the other end of the house, searching for Brock.

It was perverse, but Sam couldn't help herself.

She sat in her father's home theater (which looked like a small art-house theater in every way—twenty rows of plush seats with built-in cup holders, a full-size screen, even an old-fashioned popcorn machine in the back) and watched Monty's footage of the Anna-Ben showdown at the V Sauna Corral, over and over. The irony was not lost on her. Until very recently it would have been Ben she was staring at with longing. And now the object of her desire was Anna.

Sam bit nervously at a hangnail, ruining the hundred-dollar lavender-oil-and-beeswax-soak manicure she'd gotten at the spa. She knew she wasn't gay. At least she didn't *think* she was gay. She'd seen Cammie naked a thousand times, Cammie had the best body on the planet, and all Sam had ever felt was envy.

So why, why, why did she have to be going through this over Anna?

It was just so unfair. Anna would never in a million years be attracted to Sam. Not that Sam wanted her to be. It was just this weird thing about a kiss. Kissing Anna.

By the light of the flickering screen, Sam checked her watch. Time for the Steinbergs' party. Cammie would be there with Susan, she'd already been informed. Dee would go with her dad. Poor Dee. She was getting stranger by the day. And Anna would be escorting some young playwright/screenwriter wannabe from New York. But up on the screen, twenty-foot-tall Anna was telling off twenty-foot-tall, sweat-drenched Ben. How could Anna look so good in a simple bathing suit, hair slicked back, and no makeup? She was probably lovely even when she cried.

Shit.

Sam turned and shouted to Monty in the projection booth, "Turn it off!"

The screen went black, and the house lights came

on. "It's killer, huh?" Monty said as he stepped into the theater.

Yeah, it was. There was understated Grace Kellyesque Anna, forced into a confrontation by this gorgeous stud, Ben. She could almost hear Anna saying, "This simply is not done!" It was a fabulous illustration of the gulf between old rich and new rich. But Sam had promised Anna that she wouldn't use any of this footage for their school project. Not that Sam was above breaking a promise. It wouldn't be the first broken promise of the week or even the weekend.

The film would be so much better with the sauna showdown. And it was so tantalizing, satisfying, even, to think of everyone at school witnessing Anna's haughty kiss-off to Ben Birnbaum. If you didn't know the backstory about Ben dumping her on New Year's Eve—and no one at school knew the backstory—Anna came off like a total bitch. Of course, Anna wasn't a bitch. She was perhaps the least bitchy girl Sam knew.

But that was beside the point. It would be a simple matter for Sam to edit in this material right before they showed the film in class later in the week. It would seem to everyone like Anna had wanted it to be there— thereby giving it the most important element any work of art could have: plausible deniability. And since it was Anna's movie as well as Sam's, well . . . everyone would assume Anna had gotten cold feet at the last moment if she protested.

But the shame of it was, Sam knew she'd feel guilty

as hell. It would be so much easier if she hated Anna. *But I have to go and like her. And it's not like Anna's ready to throw her arms around me and swap spit.*

Sam made a decision. Which was not to make a decision. She'd hang on to the footage but hold off using it in the film.

For now.

Susan Needs Coffee

"So I am reading script and crying because they wish me to do shower scene, you understand?"

Justine, the tall, stunningly beautiful former Victoria's Secret model from Ukraine, droned on in Anna's ear—there was a jazz trio in one corner of the living room that made it hard for her to hear. Yet she was making all the appropriate noises of interest because Justine was an Apex client. But her mind was really on Brock. She hadn't seen him for an hour, though she'd made a real effort to find him.

"I wish to be serious artist," Justine insisted in her thick accent.

Anna couldn't quite figure out how Justine could be "serious artist" unless the role called for someone with an incomplete command of the English language, but she kept the patented pleasant smile on her face.

"So I am meeting wonderful writer at my gym," Justine went on. "He say he write part for me. Action part. Like Lara Croft, only taller."

At that moment, Anna saw Margaret step into the

living room. She wore an impeccably cut, custom-fit beige Dolce and Gabbana suit. Margaret's eyes scanned the room; Anna knew who she was looking for. Anna. Or, more correctly, Anna and Brock Franklin.

"Oh, this is Margaret Cunningham!" Justine exclaimed, waving. Since she was six foot three in her Charles David stiletto high heels, people in Fresno could have seen the wave.

Naturally, Margaret waved back.

"She is old and still has looks, you know?" Justine told Anna as Margaret gracefully worked her way toward them. "She has face-lift, you think?"

"Justine, what a pleasure to see you," Margaret said, air kissing the actress. "And our darling Anna."

Anna plastered an even more pleasant smile on her face. "Nice to see you, Margaret."

"Where's Brock?" Margaret asked.

Good question. "He'll be right back," Anna assured her.

"Yes, I suppose you couldn't very well follow him into the bathroom, could you," Margaret said agreeably. "Is he having a good time?"

"He seems to be," Anna hedged.

"Well, I'm sure you're doing a splendid job, Anna. I have complete confidence in you." Margaret gave Anna's hand a little squeeze. "I thought I'd stop by so that I could introduce Brock to some of the important people here he doesn't know. Take the pressure off you a bit, dear."

"How thoughtful," Anna managed.

"It's such a fabulous coincidence that your sister used to date him," Margaret said. "Is she here yet? I've been looking forward to meeting her, too."

"Not yet."

"She hasn't been having any . . . problems?" Margaret asked brightly.

Anna knew Margaret was referring to her sister's aborted rehab stint. "She's doing great," Anna assured Margaret.

"Excellent," Margaret said, beaming. "I'm sure this is a whole new start for her."

"She's coming with Cammie Sheppard, actually," Anna said, grateful that Margaret was being so discreet about Susan.

Margaret gave a tinkling laugh. "Clark's daughter? My, what a small world. I didn't know you girls were friends."

"We met at Jackson Sharpe's wedding." Anna offered the minimum of information necessary. "Sam Sharpe introduced us."

"Oh, I am knowing Sam!" Justine cried happily. "She is nice girl!"

Great. Everyone knew everyone, and everyone was peachy. Except for Anna, who knew she had to find Brock Franklin in the next five minutes or face the wrath of her boss. So she alluded to freshening up and headed in the direction of where a bathroom might be. As quickly as she dared, she dashed down the hallway that led to the rear grounds of the mansion, hoping against hope that she'd encounter Brock somewhere along the way.

Out back, the party had a different atmosphere: People stood around a large stone fountain, listening and dancing to live reggae music and drinking tropical beverages from half coconuts. Long tables covered in snowy white linen overflowed with Jamaican food—jerk chicken, grilled grouper, and ackee. Beautiful people mingled, laughed, talked, and tried to attract attention while at the same time pretending not to. Brock Franklin was not among them.

Just as she was about to return to the mansion, though, Anna saw her sister, Susan, in the crowd with Cammie.

Anna felt instant relief. Susan would definitely be able to help her find Brock. All she'd have to do was pull Susan off to the side, apologize again and explain the situation, and—

Susan spotted her.

"Anna! It's Anna!" she cried in a shrill voice. She threw her arms wide and ran toward her like an airplane coming in for a landing. "My baby sister!"

Anna caught her as she stumbled into her arms. The truth was on Susan's breath: her sister was drunk.

"I'm so sorry about our fight. I felt ashamed, tha's all, you know I fuckin' love you," Susan slurred, gripping Anna tight. "Hey! You having fun, Anna? Let's have some fun!"

Cammie sidled over to them. "As you can see, Anna, your big sister is in a happy mood."

"Are you responsible for this?" Anna asked rhetorically. She pictured her hands around Cammie's neck, squeezing against her windpipe.

"Me?" Cammie asked. "Don't they teach in rehab that you're only responsible for yourself?"

"Why, Cammie? I really would like to know."

"Ask Ben," Cammie said coldly.

"So this is supposed to be payback, is that it?" Anna asked. "You're sick, Cammie. You need help."

"Actually, I'm fabulous," Cammie said, giving Susan—who was trying and failing to get her hair unstuck from her lip gloss—a pointed once-over. "I'd say it's your sister who needs help right about now."

Anna kept her voice low. "And I'd say you're a cold-hearted bitch with a need to make the rest of the world as miserable as you are."

"Fuck you," Cammie said through a smile.

"Not on a bet," Anna spat. But she couldn't waste time on Cammie now. She had to get her sister out of there.

"Let's find you some coffee, Susan," Anna said, taking her sister's arm.

Susan jerked her arm away. "Don't want coffee. I just wanna have fun." She whirled back toward the reggae trio, who'd launched into Bob Marley's "One Love," and tugged Anna toward the musicians. "Come on and dance, Anna!"

Anna extricated herself. "No dancing, Susan. Let's just go inside and—"

"No! Come on!" Susan teetered toward the musicians, beckoning drunkenly to her sister as a few people smiled knowingly and pointed.

Anna locked Cammie's wrist in a viselike grip. "Listen to me, Cammie. You *will* come help me get Susan inside, in as low-key a way as possible."

"Or what?"

"Or I will make you very, very sorry," Anna promised. She couldn't recall ever threatening anyone before in her life, and she wasn't even sure how she would carry out such a threat. But she did know this: she meant it.

Cammie gave Anna's hand on her arm a withering look. "Yeah, right," she scoffed.

"Anna Cabot Percy, come on!" Susan called. She was holding her hair off her neck and spinning in a wobbly circle. "Let's dance!"

Oh God.

Anna let go of Cammie and moved toward her weaving sister but was intercepted by a woman in a crisp white blouse and black skirt who had the look of someone in charge.

"Excuse me, I'm the party planner for this affair," she said to Anna. "Do you know this girl?"

"She's my sister. Susan."

"Susan needs coffee. Let me help you."

"That would be great, thank you."

Anna and the woman approached Susan, who waved

gaily to them as she danced. "You are such a tight-ass, Anna Percy. Everyone in our family is such a tight-ass. Woo-woo!" She whirled like a dervish, then suddenly tumbled to the patio. Several guests came to her aid, and she begged them for a drink.

"You don't need a drink," Anna said, taking her by the arm.

"Yeah, I do," Susan insisted. "It's so hot out here!"

"Susan, come inside with us," the party planner told her.

Susan thrust a finger at Anna's nose. "She put you up to this, didn't she? Tha's because she's a whiner an' I'm a loser. Winner, I mean. She's the winner, *I'm* the whiner. God, it's so fucking hot."

Before Anna could stop her, Susan broke away again, running headlong toward the big stone fountain at the center of the patio. Anna got a sick feeling in her stomach. Susan wouldn't . . .

Evidently Susan would.

She leaped over the barrier ledge, dropped her pants and stepped out of them, and quickly lifted her halter top over her head. Then, clad in nothing more than a French lace thong, she jumped into the shallow fountain just as the reggae trio finished their song. Thick silence filled the air as everyone stared at the spectacle.

"Anna! Anna! What is going—?"

Anna recognized that frigid voice even as the band's next song drowned it out. One look toward the back door of the mansion confirmed her suspicion—an ashen-faced Margaret stood there with Brock, who didn't look any too steady on his feet himself.

"Hey! I know you!" the young writer bellowed to Susan, who was dancing in the fountain to music only she could hear, thong so soaked that she might as well have been naked. "You're Susan Percy! I'd recognize that ass anywhere!"

Susan whirled. "You want my ass, dickweed? Here's my—"

She never finished the sentence. Instead she keeled over, splashing the crowd as her body flopped and her head sank under the water.

That's a Wrap!

S am Sharpe stood off to one side of the rear grounds of the mansion, contemplating what to do. She'd just witnessed Susan's drunken escapade, seen the look of shock and humiliation on Anna's face as her sister tumbled into the fountain, noticed how appalled Margaret Cunningham was.

As Anna hurried to her sister's aid, Sam smiled. She knew exactly what she had to do. Thank God she'd decided to shoot some additional footage at the Steinbergs' party. And thank God she was Jackson Sharpe's daughter. When she asked the party planner whether it would be okay for her and her partner to film, the planner had said fine—so long as she might be able to get Jackson Sharpe and Poppy to make an appearance before the evening was over. Sam had assured her that this was completely possible, though in reality all she'd done was leave her father and new stepmother a note.

"Monty?" Sam spoke quietly into the tiny wireless two-way radio she always clipped to her lapel whenever she filmed at a location. "Come to the backyard. And for God's sake, point the camera at the fountain. *Now.*"

Then Sam hustled to the catering area, grabbed a spare white tablecloth, and dashed toward Anna and Susan. Anna was knee-deep in the water, her hands under her sister's soaked head, trying to reassure Susan that everything would be okay.

"Use this," Sam commanded, tossing Anna the tablecloth.

Anna caught it but looked, bewildered, at Sam. "What?"

"Don't ask questions. Just put it around your sister. Or do you want the show to continue?" Then Sam turned around, scanning the crowd for Monty. There he was, by the still-silent reggae band, camcorder whirring away. "Okay, that's a wrap!" she shouted to him.

"Got it!" Monty called back.

"This sequence is going to be fabulous," Sam told Anna in a too-loud voice as they helped a thoroughly soaked Susan from the fountain. "Your sister is a fabulous actress! Let's go get her dried off!"

Many people laughed in recognition, several even applauded as Sam turned to the crowd. "Thanks for bearing with us, for helping out some young filmmakers. Student film. Cinema verité. You were the greatest!"

Anyone who hadn't figured out what was going on was now smiling. Oh, it was a *movie* scene! To think they'd all fallen for it! And wasn't the girl at the fountain Sam Sharpe, Jackson Sharpe's daughter? She was making a film, and they had all been a part of it. How clever!

Sam cocked her chin toward the side of the mansion. "That way. Don't worry about Monty; he'll take care of himself."

Together they led Susan around the mansion and toward the parking area. Sam thrust her claim stub and a hundred-dollar bill at one of them; her Jensen materialized in a matter of seconds. They loaded Susan into the backseat, and moments later they were heading out onto Loma Vista Drive.

Back at the party, Cammie made her way to the outdoor bar for another glass of champagne. Damn Anna, anyway. Cammie's plan had worked brilliantly. But instead of humiliating Anna, all she'd accomplished was Sam-to-the-rescue. Now Anna and Sam would probably become friends or something. It really was depressing.

"Hi, Cammie," Dee said as she came up next to Cammie, orange juice in hand. "Having fun?"

"No." Cammie took the champagne from the bartender and sipped it.

"So it was really nice of Sam to save Susan like that, wasn't it?" Dee asked.

Christ. It just got worse and worse. If Dee could figure out that Sam had come to Susan's rescue, then anyone could figure it out.

"How did Susan get so wasted, anyway?" Dee asked.

"How would I know, Dee?"

"Well, I mean, she came to the party with you," Dee pointed out.

"She's an *alcoholic*," Cammie spat. "That's what alcoholics do."

"Well, yeah, but I mean, not when there's a friend around to help them make a healthier choice." Dee went wide-eyed. "You didn't get her drunk on purpose, did you? I mean, I know sometimes you act out your hostility issues, but you wouldn't do *that*, right?"

The reggae singer in the backyard wailed the line "Lead me not into temptation, sister." Cammie took a long swallow of champagne.

"I didn't lead Susan into temptation, Dee," she lied. "She got there all by herself."

"She okay?" Sam asked.

"Out cold," Anna reported.

"You okay?"

"Not really," Anna admitted. As Sam drove along on Loma Vista Drive, she could see Anna's hands were shaking. So much for the icy exterior . . . sangfroid. "Margaret Cunningham is going to kill me. But still, I don't know what to say. Thank you feels inadequate."

Sam was touched but too self-conscious to show it. She decided to go for glib. "How about, 'I owe you a tremendous debt of gratitude, which you may choose to collect at a time and place of your own choosing'?"

"That'll work. I didn't even know you were there. That was incredibly quick thinking."

"Hey, you're my friend and my partner; what are friends for, anyway? And where are we going?"

"Not the Beverly Hills Hotel. I'm sick of that place," Anna decided. "My father's house? I'll put Susan in my room."

Sam nodded and turned onto Sunset Boulevard. "At the risk of stating the obvious, it doesn't seem like rehab took."

"Cammie did this."

"What, she forced alcohol down your sister's throat?"

"You know what I mean."

"Yeah." Sam thought about it for a moment. "This is low, even by her very low standards." They rode in silence until Sam turned into the driveway and pulled to a stop by the front walkway. "Home sweet home. Let's get your sister inside."

Together they half lifted, half dragged Susan out of the car. It took five minutes of herculean effort to get her inside, up the stairs, and onto Anna's bed. There Anna rolled her off the white tablecloth and gently placed two blankets over her nude body.

"Thanks, Sam," Anna said. "Really."

"Anytime." Sam found she meant this with her whole heart. What was happening to her?

"Hopefully there won't be a repeat performance."

Susan groaned, rolled over, and scrunched her body into a fetal position. Sam had been that drunk a number of times, but the sight of Susan made her vow not to do it again. At least not anytime soon.

"Want coffee?" Anna asked.

"Sure."

They went downstairs to the kitchen, where Anna started up the Braun machine. "I'm putting off calling Margaret," Anna confessed. "It's not going to be pretty. She'll probably fire me."

"For taking care of your sister?"

"I was supposed to be there for Apex, remember?"

"Well, it's not like this internship is crucial to you. You don't even want to be in the industry, do you?"

"No," Anna said. "I don't think so, anyway."

"That's a shame," Sam told her. "Because I think you really can write. I may have minimized it in the beginning, but that was because I felt threatened. There's a lot we could do together . . . someday."

"Well, thanks for the compliment. Who knows . . . maybe I'd consider it," Anna said. "But I was going to get to meet all these writers. And read plays and movie scripts."

"Scripts?" Sam hooted in disbelief. "You want scripts? There are ten thousand of them in my dad's study. Movie scripts, play scripts, book manuscripts. From the biggest writers in the world. You want to know why? Because they all know that if they can get my father attached to their project, they'll get the movie made, and they'll make the easiest million dollars they ever made. Scripts? Come on over, you're welcome to them. But I'll tell you ahead of time, most of them suck. Which is why most movies suck."

Anna fiddled with her coffee cup as she waited for

the Braun to do its thing. "This is just not my style," she fretted. "I've never left a train wreck behind me like this. It feels terrible."

"Anna, you didn't do anything. Your sister did."

"You're right," Anna said. "I'm calling Margaret."

Anna found Margaret's cell number but only reached her voice mail. She left a brief apology, asked Margaret to return the call, and hung up. The coffee was ready, so she poured two cups and handed one to Sam. "Cream? Sugar?"

"Black."

"What a day." Anna took a sip of the steamy brew. "How about we go sit in the gazebo? It's beautiful out back, and I need to clear my mind of homicidal impulses."

They walked outside, following the backyard path to the old-fashioned gazebo. "If you let Cammie get to you, she wins, you know," Sam pointed out as they sat down.

"Why is it always about winning and losing, Sam? How can it make her feel better to hurt me? It's really sick, you know."

"Yeah, well, if it's a sickness, it's the plague of Hollywood. Besides, Cammie has some great qualities, too."

"You're *defending* her?"

Sam's eye fell on a statue of Cupid in the center of the gazebo floor; someone had placed a fresh red rose in Cupid's quiver. "Let's just say I know how much it can hurt to have a broken heart."

"So do I, but that doesn't excuse her behavior. When I look at her, all I see is hate." Anna reached over and put her hand on Sam's. "But you . . . you're a good person. You're better than Cammie. And you're too smart for Dee. You don't have to hang with them."

Sam's heart lurched. Was it possible that Anna was *responding* to her? And if she was, was it a platonic response . . . or otherwise? Sam wanted Anna to be her friend. But she also wanted Anna to kiss her. But she also did not want to be gay or even bi, despite how chic it was these days to be either of those two things. Dr. Fred could say anything he wanted to say about not acting on impulses, but just feeling what she was feeling as Anna's hand rested atop hers was enough to send her into an anxious tizzy.

Sam pulled her hand away. She could be Anna's friend, maybe. If they just didn't touch. No matter what her own body was telling her to do.

"Forget me," she said briskly. "Let's talk about you and Ben. Because there still is a you and Ben, no matter how hard you try to convince yourself that there isn't."

"Sam, he dumped—"

"Yadda, yadda, yadda, heard it a zillion times," Sam singsonged. "Don't you ever give someone the benefit of the doubt?"

"Meaning what? He told me the truth?"

"How the hell do I know? Maybe yes, maybe no. So for one night, he didn't earn an A on your daily report card of life. So what? God, you're so full of it. The real reason you're resisting is because you're afraid. Afraid you might get carried away to someplace with him that you've never gone before. Afraid he'll make you want to burn that stupid report card. I think it scares the shit out of you."

When Anna didn't answer, Sam could see that she'd hit the mark.

Anna looked around the landscaped backyard and frowned. "Funny. I came to California to get away from everything. But it feels like a whole new *everything* has followed me here."

"Yeah, well, as Dr. Fred always tells me, 'Wherever you go, Sam, there you are.'" Sam wasn't sure if she was talking about herself or about Anna. Or maybe both.

"I just want to get away. Ever feel like that?"

"All the time. But I'd miss my morning blowouts with Raymond. Kidding. Listen, why don't you do it? Get away?"

"How can I? There's Susan and Margaret and our project. . . ." Anna blinked. "That's funny. Because I just thought of the perfect place."

"Where?"

"I saw it in a magazine in the reception area at Apex. The Montecito Inn, I think it was called."

"Oh, sure, I've been there," Sam said. "It's up the coast in Santa Barbara. A little low-key for my taste, but okay."

"It looked beautiful. God, I'd love to go," Anna said wistfully.

"Just get in the car and go, then."

Anna's eyes lit up. "Yeah?"

"Yeah. But be back by Tuesday night. We've got a lot of film to edit. I took the liberty of looking at the rushes on the monologues we filmed this morning, and they were as good on the screen as they were on the page. I told you, I really do think you have a lot of talent. Anyone who can make Dee Young sound appealing has a gift."

Anna smiled. "Thanks, Sam. For everything. I really do owe you. I mean it."

"Yeah, you do. Don't worry, I'll collect." She added a smile of her own. "Give me your valet claim ticket from the party. I'll have one of my dad's flunkies bring your car back here."

Ten minutes later Sam was on her way back to the Sharpe estate in Bel Air, her thoughts tumbling over each other. Ben and Anna. Adam and Anna. Anna's claim that she didn't want to be with Ben or Adam. Sam and Anna. What Sam found herself wanting, more than anything, was to have Anna be her friend. The kind of friends that helped each other and did selfless things for each other, all in the name of friendship. Well, at least that was what happened in the movies.

Her life might not be a movie. But that didn't mean Sam Sharpe couldn't do something selfless for once in her overprivileged life. Before she could talk herself out of it, she used the hands-free dialer in her car to call a number on her cell.

Fifty Grand

Anna stayed out in the gazebo for a few minutes after Sam departed, calling Margaret again on her cell and reaching nothing but the answering machine. Then she just sat there, railing against the dying light of this bizarre Sunday.

With darkness came the chill of evening and a brisk Pacific breeze, which made her return to the house. As soon as she stepped into the kitchen, her father thundered at her. "Anna? What the hell happened?" He stood up from the table, a full brandy snifter in his hand. "And what the hell is Susan doing passed out on your bed?"

"Susan happened. She met me at the party. She was drunk. I had to get her out of there, Dad."

"Did you tell Margaret?"

"She saw me. But there wasn't time for me to talk to her."

"Well, then, I imagine you're out of an internship," Jonathan said.

"It was the right thing to do. Susan was in trouble. I'd do exactly the same thing again."

Jonathan sat back down at the table. "Margaret never should have asked your sister to go there. It's not like she didn't know she was straight out of rehab. . . . What am I saying? There I go, making excuses for her. We all make excuses for Susan."

Anna sat down opposite her dad. "For what it's worth, Susan didn't get drunk on her own."

"Someone poured booze down her throat?"

"No," Anna admitted. "At least I don't think so."

Her father rubbed his eyes. "She blames me, doesn't she?"

What was *wrong* with her family? Didn't anyone take any responsibility for anything? "Listen, Dad," Anna said, changing the subject and backing away toward the stairs. " I think I need to get away for—"

"Anna, wait."

Something in her father's voice made her stop. She folded her arms and strove for a patience she didn't feel. "What?"

"Our family is very good at avoidance," Jonathan said. "With Susan . . . when she went away to Bowdoin . . . Jeez, this isn't easy." He set his brandy snifter down on the table.

And suddenly it occurred to Anna—her father was trying to tell her something specific. About Susan.

"I knew something happened, Dad. I just never knew what it was."

"The truth is, your sister's life was in danger. She'd gotten involved with this lowlife musician," her father said. "Sex, drugs, rock and roll—the whole nine yards. If there was a problem, he had it. And he was giving it to your sister."

"Did you try to talk to her?" Anna asked.

"Endless times," Jonathan said. "She'd swear to us that she was going to end it but then never did. It was like a sickness. I mean, the guy got her hooked on I don't know what. We should have seen it for the addiction that it was."

Anna gulped. She'd never heard the details of this story before—and now she could understand why Susan was so reluctant to talk about it.

"I'm sorry," she told her father. "It must have been extremely hard for you and Mom."

"No kidding," Jonathan said. "It was like your sister was this out-of-control car, careening toward a cliff, with no steering wheel or brakes."

"Is that so?"

Anna turned. A very pale, unsteady Susan was in the doorway, supporting herself against the door frame with her hands. "An out-of-control car, without a steering wheel or brakes? I come down for a drink of water, and I get *this?*"

"It was the truth!" Jonathan said emphatically.

"It's as far from the truth as a lie can be," Susan retorted. "The *truth* is, Anna, I was crazy about Eric. Mother, of course, was appalled because he was so wildly inappropriate. She used to send me notes on her monogrammed stationery—handwritten—where she'd mention the lovely boys at Dartmouth and Williams I'd gone to school with and how they were all asking about me. It was her way of saying, 'Get rid of your loser boyfriend.' As for our dear father, he had other methods."

"Susan, it was a long time ago. There's no need to wallow in this story," Jonathan said.

"Pardon my French, Dad, but fuck it. We should have told Anna a long time ago." Susan looked at Anna again. "Mom was so upset that she asked Dad to make a trip back east to see Eric. Then Dad, in his usual diplomatic fashion, explained to Eric that he could make it worth Eric's while to drop out of my life."

It took Anna a moment to understand what Susan meant. "You mean, he paid your boyfriend to dump you?" She whirled on her father in disbelief.

"He was a scummy—"

"Oh my God, you did. How much did you pay him?"

"Does it matter?"

"I'd just like to know the going rate," Anna said coldly.

"Fifty grand. And he took it. He even told Susan about it before he left. Your mother and I did you a favor, Susan."

"Well, guess what, Dad? I think about it every time I get high. I'm worth fifty thou!"

Anna put her head in her hands. Some things were finally starting to make sense. "How long is that going to be your excuse?" their father asked defensively. "For living like a pig and hating us and drinking yourself to death?"

"How?" Anna whispered to her father. "How could you do that to her?"

"Yes, Daddy dearest," Susan said. "How could you do that to me?"

Jonathan slumped in his chair. "When you're a parent, you'll understand. For what it's worth, I'm sorry. "

Save for the metallic whine of the refrigerator, the kitchen was silent for a long time. Finally Anna said, "Look, you two. I'm going away for a day or so. I'll be back on Tuesday. In the meantime I strongly suggest you continue this conversation from Dad's 'I'm sorry' and go from there."

The Truth

The Montecito Inn was directly on the ocean, just a few miles south of Santa Barbara. As the bellboy led Anna to her suite, she could hear waves crashing and terns calling. She'd brought a single overnight case with her—it was all the baggage she had, unless you counted the emotional kind.

The bellboy cracked the windows and turned on some soft lights and the ceiling fan. Anna tipped him well; he departed. Then she lay down on one of the two queen-size beds and watched the lace curtains dance in the breeze. The suite was done in pale shades of aquamarine and blue. Above her, an old-fashioned wooden ceiling fan whirred slowly. It felt like a symbol of her life—turning, turning, but going nowhere. No clue how to separate who she was from who she was raised to be.

Funny. Hadn't Susan found herself in the same situation at just about the same point in her life? At Bowdoin she'd tried to figure out who she was, separated from her family for the very first time, until the

243

velvet noose of their parents' fortune had wound around her neck, choking the fledgling self she'd been trying to create. But wasn't making mistakes part of figuring out who the hell you were—even choosing the wrong guy? Anna thought again how out of touch her parents had always been with their daughters.

But they didn't turn your sister into an alcoholic, a voice in her head said. Anna was worried about her sister, but ultimately Susan would have to be responsible for herself. Just as Anna had to take responsibility for letting Brock wander off at the Steinbergs' party. If the internship at Apex was gone—maybe Margaret would give her another chance, maybe not—it was entirely her own responsibility.

So really—

Enough. Anna sat bolt upright. Too many thoughts! She needed to move, not think. A run on the beach was just what she needed. So Anna changed into running shoes, shorts, a T-shirt, and a Trinity sweatshirt, tied her room key to her sneakers, and left.

The night was brisk but pleasant. Anna jogged down to the water's edge. When she reached the hard sand below the high-tide line, she picked up her pace, grit crunching under her Reeboks. She hadn't gotten any exercise lately, and it felt great to push her body. She really needed to get into a ballet class, get some discipline back into her life and—

God, it was so hard for her to turn off the noise in her mind. Even when she didn't want to, she overthought everything! She forced herself to concentrate on her breathing—in, out, in, out, in, out—as she ran laps around the inn and down to the ocean.

Thirty minutes later she stopped, plopping down at the base of a lifeguard stand. She guessed she'd run three miles. She pulled off her sweatshirt, wiped it across her sweaty brow, and then dabbed at her neck.

"We can't go on meeting like this, Anna."

Anna almost jumped out of her skin. Someone—a male—was on the other side of the lifeguard stand. She thought it sounded like . . . but it couldn't possibly be . . .

But it was.

Ben came around the structure, hands shoved deep into the pockets of his jeans. He wore a blue fisherman's sweater that matched his eyes. "How's 'hi' for an opener?" he asked.

Her mind was trying to catch up with reality. He was there with her, on the beach in Santa Barbara, at midnight. "What are you . . . how did you . . . ?"

"Sam called me tonight and told me you were here," Ben said. "I saw you running when I arrived."

"Why would she do that? Call to tell you where I went?"

Ben shrugged. "I think it's called friendship."

"And I think what you're doing is called stalking," Anna said, pushing hair that had escaped from her ponytail off her sweaty face. "I came here to be alone."

"I have something to tell you. After that, you can

spend your whole life alone if you want to. I'm just so damn sick of lying."

Lying. Ben had been lying. In her heart, she'd known all along. "I'm sick of it, too, Ben. So why don't you tell me the truth?"

"You think it's easy?"

"So it isn't easy, so what? Hardly anything worth doing is easy. Why can't you just—oh, forget it!" Frustrated, she picked up a rock and flung it into the surf.

"The truth is, I wasn't with some mystery celebrity after I left you on New Year's Eve," he said. "I was on a plane to Vegas."

Las Vegas? That made zero sense.

Anna waited for him to continue. He looked straight out at the ocean as he spoke. "It wasn't some big actress who nearly died. It was my asshole of a father. He has a gambling problem. A big one. He makes a small fortune and gambles away more. My mom was the one who called me. They'd had a fight that night, and he'd driven off to Vegas to play thousand-dollar-a-hand blackjack. That was no big thing. Until my mom discovered that he'd taken a loaded pistol with him."

Anna couldn't help it. She gasped.

"She called the police—so you can check this story out if you want to. But I wasn't going to wait for the police. I went straight to LAX and flew to Vegas. Found him at the Bellagio—that's where he always stays— sixty grand in the hole. When I tried to pull him away from the table, he punched me. His plan was to either win or blow his own brains out."

Anna's hand flew to her mouth.

"Nice, family, huh?" Ben asked bitterly.

"Why didn't you just tell me?" Anna whispered into the dark.

"Because it's goddamn humiliating, that's why. And because I've kept his secrets for so many years, I hardly know how to tell the truth anymore. So now my mom's checked into the UCLA psychiatric unit for 'exhaustion'"—he raised his quote fingers, pausing in disgust—"the euphemism my family likes to use. That's why I haven't gone back to school."

So, she wasn't the reason he was still in town. A bit of a disappointment, if Anna were to be honest with herself.

"I shouldn't have left you on the boat that night, Anna," Ben went on. "But I did try to call you twice. I guess you slept through it."

"And what about the girl?" Anna asked, surprising herself. The words tumbled out of her mouth as if they had a will of their own. She'd been sure she didn't care anymore. Obviously she did.

"What girl?"

"The one on the boardwalk."

"She was my cousin. I swear. I asked her to act like my girlfriend when I saw you with Adam, and she kind of ran with it. Pretty pathetic, huh?"

Anna didn't answer. There was too much information

to sift through. She simply stood silently, drawing short lines in the sand with the toe of her sneaker.

"So, that's it," Ben said. "You don't have to say anything. Believe me, I know I ruined what we had together. Might have had, anyway. You'll never know how sorry I am about that. I won't bother you anymore. At least now I can live with myself." He turned and headed back to the inn parking lot.

"Ben, wait." She ran and caught up with him, keeping pace with him as he walked. "Thank you. For telling me, I mean."

He said nothing until the lot was in sight. "Well, better late than never, huh?"

"I know all about family secrets and putting up a perfect front. My parents are life masters at it."

"East Coast WASP version and West Coast Jewish version, huh? They're probably more alike than anyone would think." He attempted a smile and cocked his chin at a simple white Altima. "My rental. Downsizing. My mom's afraid they're going to lose the house. I don't even want to think about second semester tuition. That is, if I even do go back to Princeton this term." He pressed a button on his key chain and the car door unlocked. "Take care of yourself, Anna."

"You too."

He got into the Altima, started it, then backed out of the space. Anna's heart pounded. He was going to drive right out of her life as quickly as he'd flown into it when they'd met on the airplane. Unless she stopped him.

She jumped in front of the car. He rolled down the window and stuck his head out, a question in his eyes.

"Park," she said.

He did and got out.

"I want to show you something." Anna took him by the hand and led him to her suite. She opened the door. They stood on the threshold.

"Anna? What?"

"This." She wrapped her arms around his neck and kissed him. She could feel herself falling, falling into him, out of control, insane for a boy who was completely wrong for her.

"Are you sure?" he whispered into her hair.

A line from *Gatsby* flew into her head, something about how all human emotion becomes a commodity. And that made her think of a line from *Anna Karenina*, about the error mankind makes when it imagines that happiness depends on the realization of material desires. She couldn't remember either quote exactly. She was glad, because it allowed her to tell her own mind the same thing she said to Ben:

"Shut up."

Her parents would never approve: He came from new money, and his father had gambled all that new money away. His mother was in the midst of a nervous breakdown. His last name was Birnbaum.

Anna was sure of nothing, least of all the choice she was about to make. But as he carried her into the suite and kicked the door shut behind them, she didn't worry

about who she was or who she should be or what anyone would think. She didn't think about her decision
not to be involved with any boys right now. Or how
she'd feel after what she was about to do.

Because at that moment all Anna wanted was Ben,
and for once in her overplanned, oh-so-cautious good-
girl life, she just didn't give a damn.

Something wild and wicked is in the air.
The Carlyle triplets are about to take Manhattan by storm.

Lucky for you, Gossip Girl will be there
to whisper all their juicy secrets.

Turn the page for a sneak peek of

gossip girl
the carlyles

Created by the #1 *New York Times*
bestselling author Cecily von Ziegesar

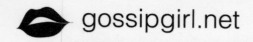

Disclaimer: All the real names of places, people, and events have been altered or abbreviated to protect the innocent. Namely, me.

hey people!

Surprised to hear from me? Don't be.

Something's happened and as you already know, I'm never quiet when things get interesting. And the Upper East Side just got a lot more exciting: We have a new threesome in town. And they're far too exquisite not to talk about . . .

But first, I'll need to back up a little.

As we all know, the beloved Avery Carlyle passed away this summer. She was the elegant, silver-haired woman who gave away her money to museums, libraries, and parks the way other people donate last season's dresses to St. Géorge's thrift shop. At seventeen, she made headlines dancing on tables. At twenty-one, she married (for the first time) and moved into the famous peach-colored townhouse on the corner of 61st and Park. And at seventy-two, she still drank Coke and Gin and was always surrounded by fresh-cut peonies. Most importantly, she was the queen of getting exactly what she wanted from anyone. A woman after my own heart.

So how does this affect me, you ask? Keep your panties on, I'm getting there. Avery Carlyle's wayward daughter, Edie—who ran away to Nantucket to find herself through art after college—was called back to New York to sort through her mother's affairs. Judging by the bookcase of leather-bound journals (and the six annulled marriages) Mrs. Carlyle left in her wake, that process may take a while. Which is why Edie shut down the Nantucket house and moved her family into **B**'s old penthouse. Since the *père* Carlyle isn't in the picture, the cozy family of four consists of mother Edie and her triplets, **A, O,** and **B.**

Meet the Carlyles: There's **O,** buff bod, golden blond hair . . . looks good so far. Then there's **A,** blond hair, blue eyes, a fairy-tale goddess robed in J.Crew. And lastly **B,** which stands for Baby. *Aw.* But just how innocent is she?

Then of course, our old friends are up to some new tricks. There's **J,** last seen drinking Tanqueray gimlets on a yacht in Sagaponack. But why was she there, when she was supposed to be doing arabesques at the Paris Opera House? Did the pressure get to her, or was she just homesick for her tycoon-in-training boyfriend, **JP**? . . . And what about the impeccably mannered **R,** swimming laps on the rooftop pool of SoHo House while his mother did a piece on summer entertaining for her television show *Tea with Lady Sterling.* We all know Lady **S** can't wait to plan his fairy-tale wedding to long-time girlfriend, **K.** But can young love endure? Especially when **K** was seen in the confessional at St. Patrick's . . . What's to confess, Kitty Cat?

What will the old crowd think of the new additions to our fair island? I, for one, can't wait to see if they sink or swim. . . .

your e-mail

Dear GG,
So, my mom went to Constance Billard like a million years ago with the triplets' mom and she told me the reason they moved here is because **A** slept with the entire island—boys and girls. And then **B** is like, this crazy brilliant genius that's mentally unstable and never washes her clothes. And **O** apparently swims up to Nantucket on the weekends in a Speedo. Is that true?
—3some

A: Dear 3,

Interesting. From what I've seen, **A** looks pretty innocent. But we all know looks can be deceiving. We'll see how brilliantly **B** does in the city. As for **O,** Nantucket's a long way away, so I doubt he can swim that far. But if he can . . . I've got one word for you: Endurance. Exactly what I look for in a man.
—GG

Q: Dear GG,

So, I just moved here and I love New York!!!!! Do you have any advice to make this year the best year ever?
—SMLLTWNGRL

A: Dear STG,

All I can say is be careful. Manhattan is a pretty small place itself, albeit much more fabulous than wherever you came from. No matter what you do, and no matter where you are, somebody is watching. And it's not going to be gossiped about in your high school cafeteria—in this town, it's bound to hit Page Six. If you're interesting or important enough to be gossiped about, that is. One can only hope.
—GG

Q: Dear GG:

I bet you're just saying you deferred from college because you didn't get in anywhere. Also, I heard that a certain monkey-owning dude never made it to West Point and I think it's pretty mysterious that he's still here and so are you. Are you really a girl?? Or are you even a senior? I bet you're just some nerdy thirteen-year-old.
—RUCHUCKB

A:
Dear RUCHUCKB,

I'm flattered that my continued presence is spawning conspiracy theories. Sorry to disappoint, but I am as feminine as they come, without a pet monkey in sight. My age? As the venerable elder Avery Carlyle would say: A real lady never tells.
—GG

Sightings

This just in, from the newbies: **O** running in **Central Park,** without a shirt. Does he own any shirts? Let's hope not! . . . **A** trying on a silver sequined Marni minidress in the dressing room of **Bergdorf**'s. Didn't anyone tell her Constance has a dress code? . . . And her sister **B** in **FAO Schwartz,** clinging to a guy in a barn-red NANTUCKET HIGH hoodie putting stuffed animals in inappropriate poses and taking pictures. Is *that* what they do for fun where they're from?

Okay, ladies and gents, you all probably have to go back-to-school shopping—or for those of you who've headed off to college, read Ovid and chug a beer in your new 8 x 10 dorm room. But don't worry; I'll be here, drinking a glass of Sancerre at Balthazar, reporting on what you're missing. It's the dawn of a new era on the Upper East Side, and with these three in town, I just know it's going to be another wild and wicked year. . . .

You know you love me,

gossip girl

welcome to the jungle

Baby Carlyle woke up to the sound of garbage trucks beeping loudly as they backed up Fifth Avenue. She rubbed her puffy eyelids and set her bare feet on the red bricks of her family's new terrace, pulling her boyfriend's red Nantucket High sweatshirt close to her skinny frame.

Even though they were all the way on the top floor, sixteen stories above Seventy-second and Fifth, she could hear the loud noises of the city coming to life below. It was so different from her home in Nantucket, where she used to fall asleep on the beach with her boyfriend, Tom Devlin. His parents ran a small bed-and-breakfast, and he and his brother had lived in a guest cottage on the beach since they were thirteen. He'd come to visit for the weekend, and after he left last night, Baby dragged a quilt onto the terrace's hammock and fell asleep in a Frette duvet cocoon.

Note: Sleeping al fresco is a worst-case-scenario situation. Never done willingly (i.e., only if your cruise ship hits an iceberg or your elephant loses a leg on safari).

Baby shuffled through the sliding French doors and into the cavernous apartment she was now expected to call home.

The series of large rooms, gleaming hardwood floors and ornate marble detail was the opposite of comfortable. She dragged the duvet behind her, mopping the spotless floors as she wound her way to her sister Avery's bedroom.

Inside, Avery's golden-blond hair was strewn across her pale pink pillow, and she sounded like a broken teakettle. Baby pounced on the bed.

"Hey!" Avery Carlyle sat up and pulled the strap of her white Cosabella tank top. Her long blond hair was matted and her blue eyes were bleary, but she still looked regally beautiful, just like their grandmother had been. Just like Baby wasn't.

"It's morning," Baby announced, bouncing up and down on her knees like a four-year-old high on Sugar Smacks. She was trying to sound perky, but her whole body felt heavy. It wasn't just that her whole family had uprooted themselves from Nantucket last week, it was that New York City had never—*would never*—feel like home.

When Baby was born, her emergence had surprised her mother, and the midwife, who thought Edie was only having twins. While her brother and sister were named for their maternal grandparents, the unexpected third child had simply been called Baby on her birth certificate. The name stuck. Whenever Baby had come to New York to visit her grandmother, it was clear from Grandmother Avery's sighs that while twins were acceptable, three was an unruly number of children, especially for a single mother like Edie to handle. Baby was always too messy, too loud, too much for Grandmother Avery's presence, too *much* for New York.

Now, Baby wondered if she might have been right. Everything, from the boxy rooms in the apartment to the grid of New York City streets, was about confinement and order. She sighed and bounced on her sister's bed some more and Avery groaned sleepily.

"Come on, wake up!" Baby urged, even though it was barely ten, and Avery always liked to sleep in.

"What time is it?" Avery sat up in bed and rubbed her eyes. She couldn't believe she and Baby were related. Baby was always doing ridiculous things, like teaching their dog, Chance, to communicate by blinking. It was as if she were perpetually stoned. But even though her boyfriend was a raging stoner, Baby had never been into drugs.

It doesn't really sound like she needs them.

"It's after ten," Baby lied. "Want to go outside? It's really pretty," she cajoled. Avery looked at Baby's puffy brown eyes, and knew immediately that she'd been crying over her loser boyfriend all night. Back in Nantucket, Avery had done everything possible to avoid Tom. This past weekend, it had been impossible. Even though their apartment took up half the top floor of the building, it wasn't large enough to escape his grossness. Every day, she'd found something more disgusting about him, from the stained white Gap athletic socks he'd ball up and give to their cat, Rothko, to play with, to the one time she had walked in on him wearing Santa Claus–print boxers and doing bong hits on the terrace. She knew Baby liked that he was *authentic*, but did authentic have to mean appalling?

Short answer? No.

"Fine, I'll come outside." Avery pulled herself out from under her 600-thread count Italian cotton sheets and walked barefoot onto the terrace, and Baby followed. Avery squinted her eyes in the bright sunlight. Below her, the wide street was empty except for an occasional sleek black towncar whooshing down the avenue. Beyond the street was the lush expanse of Central Park, where Avery could just barely make out the tangled maze of paths winding through its greenery.

The two sisters sat together, swinging in the hammock and overlooking the other landscaped Fifth Avenue terraces and balconies, empty except for the occasional rooftop gardener. Avery sighed in contentment. Up here, she felt like the Queen of the Upper East Side, which was exactly what she was born to be.

Was she really?

"Hey." Owen Carlyle, six foot two and shirtless, stepped onto the terrace carrying a carton of orange juice, a bottle of champagne, and wearing just a Speedo, a maroon towel knotted around his slim hips. Avery rolled her eyes at her swimming-obsessed brother, who could easily drink anyone under the table and then beat them in a 10K.

"Mimosa anyone?" He took a swig of orange juice from the carton and grinned at Avery's repulsed grimace. Baby shook her head sadly as her tangled hair brushed against her shoulder blades. Always tiny, Baby now looked absolutely fragile. Her tangled brown hair had already lost the honey highlights that always showed up during the first weeks of a Nantucket summer.

"What's up?" he asked his sisters companionably.

"Nothing," Avery and Baby answered at the same time.

Owen sighed. His sisters had been so much easier to under-stand when they were ten, before they'd started acting all coy and mysterious. If girls weren't so irresistible in general, he might have given them up and become a monk. Case in point: The only rea-son he was up so early was the semi-pornographic dream that had forced him out of bed and on an unsuccessful hunt for a pool.

Dream about whom? Details please.

He placed the unopened bottle of champagne in a large daisy-filled planter and took another swig of OJ before squishing into the hammock next to his sisters. He glanced down at the mass of trees, not believing how small Central Park seemed. From up here, everything looked miniaturized. He just wished he had an expanse of dark ocean in front of him, like he'd had back in Nantucket.

"Helloooooo!" The sound of their mother's voice and the jangling of her handcrafted turquoise and silver bracelets carried out onto the terrace from inside. Edie Carlyle appeared in the French doorway. She wore a blue Donna Karan sundress, and her normally blond-streaked-with-gray bob had been knotted into a hundred tiny braids. She looked like a scared porcupine rather than a resident of Manhattan's most exclusive zip code.

"I'm so glad you're all here," she began breathily. "I need your opinion on something. Come, it's inside." She gestured toward the foyer, her chunky bracelets clanking against each other.

Avery giggled as Owen dutifully slid off the hammock and wavered into the apartment, following Edie's long stride. For the past week, Owen had been acting as Edie's de facto art adviser. He had been to an opening almost every night, usually in an overcrowded, patchouli-ridden gallery in Brooklyn or Queens where he drank warm Chardonnay and pretended to know what he was talking about.

The expansive, wood-paneled rooms that had once housed toile Louis XIV Revival chaises and Chippendale tables were now empty except for a few cast-offs Edie had found through her extensive network of artist friends. Avery had immediately ordered a whole ultramodern look from Jonathan Adler and Celerie Kempbell, but the furniture hadn't yet arrived. In the interim Edie had managed to find an orange moth-eaten couch to place in the center of the living room. Rothko was furiously scratching at it, his favorite new activity since moving to New York. Most of their pets—three dogs, six cats, one goat, and two turtles—had been left in Nantucket. Rothko was probably lonely.

Not for long.

Sitting next to Rothko was a two-foot-high plaster chinchilla, painted aquamarine and covered in bubble wrap.

"What do you think?" Edie asked, her blue eyes twinkling. "A man was selling it for 50 cents on the street down in Red Hook when I was coming home last night from a performance. This is authentic, New York City found art," she added, rapturous.

"I'm out of here," Avery announced, backing away from the plaster sculpture as if it were contaminated. "Baby and I are going to Barneys," she decided, locking eyes with her sister and willing her to say yes. Baby had been moping around in Tom's stupid sweatshirt all weekend. It had to stop.

Baby shook her head, pulling the barn-red sweatshirt tighter against her body. She actually kind of liked the chinchilla. It looked just as out of place in the ornate apartment as she felt. "I have plans," she lied. She'd decide what those plans were just as soon as she was out of her family's sight.

Owen gazed at the statue. One of the chinchilla's heavily lidded eyes looked like it was winking at him. He really needed to get out of the house.

"I, uh, need to pick up some swim stuff." He vaguely remembered getting an e-mail saying he needed to pick up his uniform from the team captain at St. Jude's, his new school. "I should probably get to it."

"Okay," Edie trilled, as Avery, Owen, and Baby scattered to opposite ends of the apartment. School started tomorrow and all three knew it was the dawn of a new era.

Edie tenderly carried the chinchilla sculpture into her art studio. "Have fun on your last day of freedom!" she called, her voice echoing off the walls of the apartment.

Like they don't *always* have fun?

gossip girl
the carlyles

Welcome to Poppy.

A poppy is a beautiful blooming red flower
(like the one on the spine of this book). It is also
the name of the new home of your favorite series.

Poppy takes the real world and makes it
a little funnier, a little more fabulous.

Poppy novels are wild, witty, and inspiring.
They were written just for you.

So sit back, get comfy, and pick a Poppy.

poppy
www.pickapoppy.com

gossip girl

THE A-LIST   THE CLIQUE

the it girl   POSEUR